:lp us Rate this book...
ut your initials on the
ft side and your rating
   on the right side.

1 = Didn't care for
2 = It was O.K.
3 = It was <u>great</u>

9/19

DATE DUE

	OCT 15 2019		
	OCT 25 2019		
	JAN 02 2020		

DISCARDED

Initials	Rating			
_____	1 2 3			
_____	1 2 3			
_____	1 2 3			
_____	1 2 3			
_____	1 2 3			
_____	1 2 3			
_____	1 2 3			
_____	1 2 3			
_____	1 2 3			
_____	1 2 3			
_____	1 2 3			
_____	1 2 3			
_____	1 2 3			
_____	1 2 3			

PRINTED IN U.S.A.

Note: The views of the characters in this novel do not necessarily reflect the views of the author, nor is their behavior necessarily being condoned.

"Two are better than one,
because they have a good return for their labor:
If either of them falls down,
one can help the other up.
But pity anyone who falls
and has no one to help them up."
Ecclesiastes 4:9-10

CHAPTER 1

"Come over here, and let me hug you, sweetheart."

Jillian's entire body stiffened as her aunt enfolded her in an embrace that smelled suspiciously like goat.

I still can't believe I'm living on a farm.

Jillian pulled away.

What am I doing back in Orchard Grove?

Connie chuckled, easily hoisting Jillian's two suitcases toward the attic stairs. "Is this all you packed? I sure hope you didn't leave anything important back home."

What was there Jillian could have forgotten? It wasn't like she'd need anything fancy out here in the middle of nowhere. Only one thing could be worse than living in Orchard Grove with her Aunt Connie, and that was staying in Seattle with her parents.

Connie led her into the tiny attic room that had been the pirate ship, the castle, the theater, and the art studio of Jillian's childhood years — years of imagination and excitement living so close to Grandma Lucy's farm.

It wasn't that long ago really, but for Jillian it may as well have been a lifetime.

"Do you feel all right, hon?" Connie asked with that special, condescending knowing in her voice. "Can I get you anything? A glass of water maybe? You don't want to get dehydrated."

Ugh. That's why Jillian most hated the thought of living here. Hated it almost as much as the idea of staying in Seattle. Hadn't she known it would happen like this if she came to stay at Safe Anchorage Farm, her aunt fussing and making a big scene?

"I'm fine." It wasn't worth jumping straight into an argument her first night here. The long drive over the North Cascades had been tedious enough. Jillian was surprised she made it all the way to the attic without Connie making her memorize and recite a whole bunch of house rules.

She was an adult, but her aunt would always think of her as a child.

Connie stood there, looking helpless. If Jillian had to guess, she'd say her aunt was trying to come up with a way to broach the incredibly awkward subject of what had caused Jillian to get kicked out of her parents' home in the first place. That or she really had to use the bathroom but didn't want to appear rude.

Jillian turned her back to her aunt and hoisted her suitcases onto the bed. Some little old ladies collected dolls or trinkets. Here at Connie's, Grandma Lucy's prayer shawls and blankets lay in every room. Some grannies baked pies or tended flower gardens. Grandma Lucy spent her days talking to God.

At least Grandma Lucy was asleep. Jillian didn't know exactly what kind of lecture her grandmother might have in store for her, but tomorrow morning was soon enough to find out.

A goat bleated outside.

"Oh, that's Peaches. I'm coming, you old thing." Connie called out as if the goat were a child waiting at the bottom of the stairs and not an animal who was (hopefully) locked up outside in its pen where it belonged. Jillian hadn't stayed at the Safe Anchorage Farm in years, but she knew enough to expect that bright and early, Connie would come in and invite her to go out and milk the goats, a job that could take over an hour and a half start to finish.

It had been her favorite part of her summers growing up.

Now she was just tired.

Tired and ready to drown her anxieties in dreamless sleep.

Tomorrow would come all too soon, with its share of awkward conversations and forced reunions.

Tonight she was glad for the chance to be alone once Connie bustled out the door, calling to the whining goat as she hurried down the stairs.

CHAPTER 2

It's not what you think ...

I swear I'd never hurt you ...

Now look at what you made me do.

Jillian woke up with a start. The old T-shirt she'd been sleeping in clung to her sweaty skin.

She took in a deep, choppy inhale.

Breathe. Everything would be all right if she could simply find her breath.

There. It was back. She felt her cheeks.

Dry. Which meant she'd only been crying in her sleep. Maybe that was progress.

She glanced at the clock. A few minutes after four in the morning. The funny thing was Connie would probably be waking up in an hour to do her morning chores and get a head-start on her day at the farm.

As much as Jillian had loved this place as a child, she was a city girl now. Orchard Grove was no place for her.

Yet here she was.

She sat up in bed, running her hands through her hair to see how knotted it was. She'd been thrashing around so much lately she sometimes woke up and looked like her mom's honeymoon pictures from the eighties with her hair teased. Why anyone from any decade would voluntarily tangle their own hair was a mystery Jillian would likely never solve.

At least these tangles weren't too bad. Nothing a few minutes with a brush couldn't fix. The problem was she'd been too tired last night to unpack, and even in the spring, the attic was cold enough that she hated to think of freeing herself from her pile of Grandma Lucy's prayer shawls and quilts.

She made a few valiant attempts to fall back to sleep before jumping out of bed and pulling on some sweatpants and socks. She was dying of thirst, which wasn't too uncommon after these sorts of nightmares.

She felt her way gently down the stairs, each one slightly uneven in the home her grandfather had built by hand. Skipping the one step in the middle that always creaked, she relied on decade-old memories to help her grope her way to the kitchen where she was forced to turn on the light over the sink.

Water. A full, refreshing cup, a trip to the bathroom, and then maybe her brain would decide to drift back to sleep.

But if personal history was anything to rely on, she shouldn't set her hopes too high.

She reached for one of the crystal glasses. Here at Safe Anchorage, her aunt and grandmother had no concept of plastic or generic. Everything was dainty, costly, and fragile, even back when Jillian had been a clumsy kid who broke her fair share of teacups. Fortunately, Grandma Lucy was a saint in just about every definition of the word and never scolded her for her numerous accidents.

If only other Christians were that forgiving.

Jillian filled up her goblet and drank the water down. That was one thing she could appreciate about life at Safe Anchorage. Fresh, clean well water. She guzzled her first serving and turned on the faucet for a refill.

"I thought you might be awake." The warbling voice was unmistakable.

She'd hoped to go back to sleep rather than engage in conversation, especially the kind of conversation she knew must be coming up, but Jillian's heart still quickened slightly at the sound of Grandma Lucy's voice, her spirit swelling with memories of her summers spent here in

Orchard Grove, memories of simple and happy times long before life turned so chaotic.

Her grandmother stepped forward, wrapping her arms around Jillian's neck, declaring, "You've gotten so tall. I can hardly reach you."

"You say that every time I see you," Jillian reminded her.

Grandma Lucy smiled. "And each time it's just as true."

"Well, I'm done growing now." Jillian pulled away. There were so many things Grandma Lucy still didn't know, didn't realize about the past several years. So much time had passed ...

"Did you have a hard time sleeping?" Grandma Lucy asked, and without waiting for Jillian to answer, went on to add, "I had a feeling you were up."

Of course. Grandma Lucy's bizarre premonitions and *stirrings* as she sometimes called them were infamous in these parts. Neither Jillian's strictly conservative religious upbringing nor her passing knowledge of secular science could explain her grandmother's uncanny intuition.

Grandma Lucy took her by the hand. For a woman so wrinkled, her skin was remarkably soft.

Maybe all those goat soaps and lotions they made here

at Safe Anchorage really worked.

Without another word, Grandma Lucy led Jillian into the farmhouse's only modern addition, which had served as a greenhouse, a sunroom, and a place to serve guests tea, but was most commonly known as Grandma Lucy's prayer room. Here Jillian's grandmother would spend hours a day alternately reading her Bible, talking out loud to God, humming hymns or making up songs to sing to her Creator, and napping in her giant rocking chair.

Ever since she'd solidified her plans to move back to Orchard Grove, Jillian had foreseen this meeting, this conversation right here in this room. Without waiting to be told, she sat in the overstuffed chair across from Grandma Lucy's famous prayer rocker and waited for whatever lecture or interrogation was coming her way.

Her hands felt clammy, but otherwise she wasn't nervous. After all, she'd had a week to mentally rehearse the whole conversation, starting with the part where Grandma Lucy told her how worried she was for the state of Jillian's soul, how she questioned her eternal destiny and prayed for her salvation.

As if what had happened to Jillian was enough to kick her out of the kingdom of heaven for good.

Jillian had practically been raised inside the church,

sitting every Sunday, and most other nights of the week, in uncomfortable pews. She was a preacher's kid, after all. Church had been the one constant in her life.

Until even that was stripped from her.

"Well, now." Grandma Lucy eased herself into her rocker with a groan. She looked just like she had a decade ago when she'd sit Jillian in this exact same chair to practice memory verses. Grandma Lucy placed her hand on Jillian's knee, the touch somehow transmitting far more heat than was to be expected on a morning as chilly as this.

She smiled serenely, as if Jillian had been the one to call this meeting and Grandma Lucy was simply waiting patiently for her granddaughter to start the discussion.

Casting nervous glances around the room, Jillian wondered where she should start. How much did Grandma Lucy already know?

And how much more wretched and guilty would she feel after their conversation was over?

CHAPTER 3

"Ricky!" Mom called from the doorway to the garage. "Get out here now, or we're going to be late."

Grabbing Mom's purse, which she'd left on the counter, checking to make sure the car keys were still in his pocket, and adjusting his pants, which were practically falling off since he'd lost his belt, Ricky made his way to the car.

Mom was already in the passenger seat with a sour pucker on her face. "We'll be late."

Ricky glanced to make sure the garage door was actually open before he backed up. The last time he'd been in this much of a rush, he'd made a thousand-dollar mistake, so he was always careful now to double-check.

Safety before speed, as Mom would say.

Of course, this was the same woman who was at the moment complaining so loudly you'd think they must be half an hour behind schedule.

Well, as much as Mom was griping about it, they weren't late. There was no reason to worry about traffic in Orchard Grove on a Saturday morning. Ricky would bet his entire paycheck, small as it was, that they'd be at least a few minutes early.

But of course, there was no reason to try to convince Mom of that. All that was left to do was apologize for his tardiness, tell her how hard he'd work not to let something like this happen again, and keep his eyes on the road like a good, conscientious driver.

A courteous driver is a righteous driver, and all that other junk Mom quoted.

She yanked down the visor to block out the morning sun streaming in through the windshield. "What's it doing so light out today?"

It was less than four minutes later when he pulled in front of the Orchard Grove Family Medical Center and jumped out to open his mother's door for her. "What time do you think you'll be done?" he asked.

She let out a loud, noisy sigh as he reached in for her purse.

"I couldn't tell you, son. You never know with these doctors how long these appointments will take. It could be ten minutes, or maybe he'll find something wrong and have to spend hours. You better plan to come back around eleven."

By which he knew she meant no later than quarter 'til.

"I'll be here." He hurried ahead to open the door to the medical center. "Want me to walk with you up to the office?"

"I'm not an invalid yet." She reached out her hand and pressed the elevator button.

Ricky waited until the doors opened, then gave her a quick kiss good-bye. "I'll just be running a couple errands, so I'll see you soon. Have a good appointment."

"I might," she sighed as she got onto the elevator, "unless he finds out that I have a cyst or the cancer's returned."

Ricky didn't bother to mention that chiropractors probably weren't in the business of diagnosing cysts or cancer, but then again, what did he know? His mother was a walking medical encyclopedia. She could stub her toe and diagnose herself with colon cancer a minute later.

Stepping outside into the bright sunshine, Ricky smiled. There was something about spring — and having nearly an hour before he had to chauffeur his mother anywhere — that made him feel optimistic.

The feeling you get after you just completed your last

homeschool test of the year or when the girl you're crushing on just agreed to meet you at the prom.

Of course, those were distant memories now. He shouldn't dwell on them. After all, he had errands to run. This weekend was the third-year anniversary of Mom's victory over breast cancer, and even though she never said anything outright, she'd left enough hints that Ricky knew she was expecting some special way to honor the occasion. He'd already made reservations for a fancy Sunday lunch tomorrow at the Main Street Hotel, and he wanted to run by the Safe Anchorage gift shop to pick up some of those handmade goat lotions and candles she liked so much as a present.

A godly gentleman should always be considerate, giving, and generous. How many times had Mom crammed those words into his brain until they were permanently branded into his psyche?

Considerate, giving, and generous. Like the son who buys his mother fancy gifts and takes her out for an expensive brunch to celebrate three years cancer-free.

Considerate, giving, and generous. He could recite those words in his sleep. Hadn't Mom always said that's what would make him a good husband? However, based on his own pitiful track record in romance, he wasn't so sure that *considerate, giving, and generous* were the most sought-after traits in a man.

How about *strong, handsome, and muscular*? What would be so wrong with that?

CHAPTER 4

"Now remember, the goats can sense when you're nervous, so it's important to be calm and gentle." Connie patted the rump of the spotted Nubian she'd just brought up to the milking stand. "See how she's kicking? That means she's feeling a little uncomfortable."

You and me both, goat, Jillian thought.

It was still early morning, but she was exhausted. She had spent over an hour and a half in the prayer room before Grandma Lucy finally dozed off to sleep, but not before inviting Jillian to pray with her over the dozens of photo albums she kept in a pile next to her prayer chair.

Jillian never understood how that woman could talk so long. Jillian had no problems with the short, simple kind of prayers her family offered around the dinner table, but her version of *saying grace* was like a child's crude stick figure and Grandma Lucy's was a Michelangelo masterpiece.

Maybe Jillian would have turned into a prayer warrior like that. She'd certainly been spiritual enough as a kid that she might have carried that fervor into her adult life if things hadn't turned out the way they did.

"Don't hold too low now or you'll squeeze off the milk." Connie repositioned Jillian's hands on the udders. They were milking later than normal since Connie was taking time to walk her through each and every step. Jillian felt about as patient as the swollen goat to get the barn chores over and done with.

I knew this would happen if I moved back here.

When she and her family left for Seattle, she'd sworn to never step foot in this wretched part of Washington state again. Of course, having her grandmother living here made it hard to avoid Orchard Grove entirely, but aside from Christmases and other major family events, Jillian was done with this stupid town.

Or at least that's what she had thought.

Yet another one of life's unexpected twists. God was probably laughing his head off.

At least she was away from her parents, but in some ways she'd just traded in one set of conservative, judgmental guardians for another.

Grandma Lucy hadn't talked about what brought Jillian

back to Safe Anchorage Farm this morning in the prayer room. She didn't give the lecture Jillian had prepared for, but what did that matter? Even if she didn't say how disappointed she was, Jillian knew it anyway.

As if she were the first pastor's kid who ever fell off the deep end. Some people were so stupid and arrogant. Closed-minded fools who lived in a world where children were sold into slavery, teens were dying from drug overdoses, terrorists were strapping bombs to themselves and blowing up crowded buses filled with innocent civilians, and folks acted as if one tiny indiscretion was enough to send the entire world to its destruction.

So Jillian had started dating someone she shouldn't have. The way her parents treated it, she would have been better off joining the Taliban as long as she *kept herself pure* in the process.

Ridiculous. Here she was, a grown adult in the twenty-first century, and her parents were so scandalized they sent her off to an entirely different part of the state. It wasn't like they were living in Victorian England where girls were quietly and conveniently put away in situations like this. It wasn't like Jillian was the first or the last pastor's daughter to find herself pregnant out of wedlock.

But conservative Christianity was her birthright, as

much a part of her biological makeup as her strawberry blonde hair or her sunophobic complexion. She couldn't cut that part of her upbringing out of her any more than she could scrub off the small freckles that spotted her cheekbones. Her parents acted as if her *departure from the faith* happened the moment she decided to date that no-good-loser-turned-boyfriend-turned-ex-boyfriend-turned-stalker.

As if she could have known the kind of person he was back then.

As if the moment she agreed to dance with him when she went out with her friends, God removed his Holy Spirit from her, branded her a backslidden believer beyond any hope of redemption, and condemned her soul to hell.

"I think she's dry now. We better get her down and keep moving along." Connie gave a half-hearted chuckle. "It might be lunchtime before we're done."

Jillian sat on the milking stool while her aunt got the spotted Nubian down and led forward a large goat with an almost pinkish coat. "Say good-morning to Peaches."

Did her aunt expect her to remember each and every one of their dozens of goats' names? Did she seriously think Jillian cared?

"Peaches is a sweet one. Uncle Dennis sometimes calls

her my puppy goat because she'll follow me around the entire yard if I let her, just like she was a dog." She patted the animal gently between the ears and crooned sweetly to her in a babyish voice.

Jillian sighed as she washed the udder. At least Peaches wasn't as skittish as the Nubian had been.

Connie handed her a new pail. "I'm going to take what we've already got into the house and be right back. Just holler if you need anything, but I'm sure Peaches won't give you any trouble at all. She's a good girl, isn't she? Isn't she?" Connie puckered up her lips and brought her face so close to the goat's, for a moment Jillian thought she was going to kiss it.

No wonder her aunt always smelled like goats.

Connie bustled out of the barn, a pail of milk swinging from each hand.

Her back aching from hunching over, Jillian leaned her head against the animal's slightly swollen belly.

"All right, Peaches," she whispered, wondering how long it would be until she started baby-talking to the goats just like her aunt. "Let's see what you've got for us today."

CHAPTER 5

Ricky always enjoyed the drive out to Baxter Loop, or at least he enjoyed it when he had the car entirely to himself.

He turned the radio onto scan, listened to two full cycles, and finally ended up on the oldies station Mom always listened to anyway.

What kind of gift should he find for his mom? She always liked the things from the Safe Anchorage gift shop, but he'd already given her four scented candles and two new goat milk lotions for her birthday last month.

Oh, well. If Connie was there this morning, she'd help him pick out something appropriate, and if it was one of the other workers instead, he could always browse through all the jewelry.

His mom was always asking him when he'd find a girl to date, but if having a girlfriend was even half as expensive as taking care of his mother, at his current pay scale he could afford to date once he hit fifty and might consider getting married when he was a senior citizen.

It could have been simpler. Susannah Peters, his best friend since they were toddlers and his longtime crush, had recently gotten married to some missionary from the East Coast. Ricky had been more than a little disappointed — devastated might be a better word for it — but his reaction wasn't nearly so vehement as his mom's or her friends from the Women's Missionary League. In their minds, it was bad enough Susannah chose to marry less than a year after her mother's death. It was even worse to marry someone she'd met in that nebulous, shady region known in some seedy circles as *online*.

Ricky was happy for Susannah, who from the time they were both twelve years old and attended the same junior high winter retreat wanted nothing else but to become a missionary. Secretly Ricky had always hoped he might be able to change her mind and convince her to settle down in Orchard Grove, but there was no denying that she and her new husband were perfect for each other.

It was after Susannah's wedding that his mother grew even more insistent and pestered him about finding a girlfriend.

"It's a pity about that Peters girl." From the moment Susannah announced her engagement to a man no one at Orchard Grove Bible Church had ever heard of, Susannah had become nothing more than *that Peters girl*.

"It's a pity she didn't realize what a fine, godly husband you would make," Mom sighed dramatically. "Well, it's her loss, not yours."

Which never made much sense to Ricky since Susannah was the one happily married and he was the one still single.

He pulled up in front of the Safe Anchorage Farm gift shop. It was early enough that there were no other vehicles here. He'd probably be Connie's first customer of the day, and if he was lucky she'd have some cinnamon rolls or other tasty treats left over from breakfast.

He got out of the car, nearly losing his balance when his arm got stuck in the seatbelt, and checked his watch to make sure he still had plenty of time to shop for his gift and still make it back to the chiropractor's in time to pick up Mom.

CHAPTER 6

Either her aunt was right and there was something special about this goat, or Jillian was already starting to lose her mind after less than a full weekend in Orchard Grove.

"You're a pretty thing, aren't you?" She stroked Peaches' side. Her fur wasn't soft — as far as Jillian knew, there was no such thing as a fluffy goat — but her body was warm, and Jillian could almost swear the animal would wag her tail when Jillian rubbed a certain spot. The milking had gone well, but Jillian didn't know how to get her out of the stand.

"Are you itchy?" She scratched gently, and Peaches swayed her back half. The motion reminded Jillian of the way Grandma Lucy would shut her eyes and rock her body back and forth in the throes of her prayerful passion.

"That feels good, doesn't it?" She couldn't remember if Peaches was one of the goats her aunt told her was pregnant or not. "You got a baby in there making you uncomfortable, pretty mama?"

She shook her head, envisioning herself at her aunt Connie's age, coming out here every morning and sweet-talking to all the animals.

I've got to get back to the city.

As soon as she stopped scratching, Peaches stomped her foot and let out a snort of complaint. Jillian held onto the milk pail, afraid the goat might knock it over.

"Okay, okay. I'm sorry. I'll pet you some more, you spoiled little thing."

"Hey, that's no way to talk to your favorite animal, is it?"

The voice from the barn entrance startled her. "Oh!" Her quick movement spooked the goat. Peaches kicked the pail and sent warm goat milk spilling onto Jillian's lap and running down her legs.

"I'm so sorry. I didn't mean to do that. I thought you were Connie."

"Do I sound like Connie?" It was hard to say which was more irritating, the warm milk soaking into her jeans or the fact that someone had overheard her talking to one of the animals like some crazy goat lady.

She stood up with a half turn, straightening up the pail — as if there had been any milk in there left to salvage.

"I'm so sorry," The tall, lanky intruder started unbuttoning his flannel overshirt. "Here, I don't have any towels, but you can use this. I had no idea Connie hired someone to do her milking."

Jillian wasn't exactly sure how a single flannel shirt was supposed to help her clean up, but she dragged it across her legs for show and handed it back to him. "She didn't hire me. I'm her niece, and she was just teaching me how to do it."

The stranger had his head cocked to the side and was staring at her. Great. She knew exactly what was coming next.

"Jillian? Is that really you?"

If there was any possible way she could have denied it, she would have. "Yeah. Who are you?"

"It's me." he stared at her expectantly. "Me," he repeated as if she hadn't heard his unhelpful declaration the first time. "Ricky Fields."

"Oh." What else was there for her to say?

"You don't remember me, do you?"

"No, I remember you just fine. You're that guy from church." It was as safe an answer as any.

"Yeah. That's me."

"Ricky, did you say?"

His expression dropped. "You really don't remember me."

She shrugged. "It was a long time ago."

He stared at the dirty flannel in his hand. "Yeah, it was. But now that you're here, how have you been doing? Last I heard your family was out in Seattle. When did they all get back?"

"They didn't," she answered. "It's just me."

"Oh, I guess that makes sense. Because you're older now and stuff."

Was this guy for real? "Yeah," she replied. "And stuff."

Apparently lost to her sarcasm, he leaned over and gave her a hug that was one part shoulder and one part chin, emphasized by a single pat. "Well, it's really good to have you back. Where's Connie, by the way? I came to grab something for my mom at the gift shop, but it wasn't open yet."

"Yeah, we're having something of a late start this morning." As if he couldn't very clearly see that for himself.

The spilled milk had soaked into her socks. She needed a shower and a change of clothes and then a plane ticket to anywhere that wasn't Orchard Grove.

Where was her aunt?

"Hey," she said, "do you know how to get the goat out of this thing?"

"Yeah, let me show you." He reached out and scratched Peaches between the ears just like Connie had earlier. Leaning down, he crooned, "Aren't you a good little girl? Did you make lots of yummy milk today? Who's a good goaty goat. You are."

Jillian rolled her eyes. Six more months until her due date.

Six more months stuck here in Orchard Grove so her family didn't have to deal with the shame of her baby bump that would soon inflate to the size of a beach ball.

Six more months trying to keep her sanity while she was surrounded by a herd of goats and the idiots who loved them.

CHAPTER 7

"You're late. Didn't I tell you to be here by 10:30?"

Ricky held his arm out to keep the elevator doors from closing shut on his mom.

"You said eleven."

"Oh, did I? Well, you're still late."

"It's 10:45."

Mom acted as if she hadn't heard, and Ricky hurried to get in front so he could hold the door open on their way out of the medical center. "How did your appointment go?"

Mom shrugged. "I'm not planning to die anytime soon if that's what you're asking."

Inside the car, she turned down the volume on the radio and scowled. "What did you do with yourself all morning?"

"I just went down to see what Connie had at the gift shop. Did you know her niece is back in town? You remember Pastor Joel's daughter, don't you?"

"He's no pastor of mine."

"Yeah, I remember something weird about that family, but I never got what the problem was. I just remember they left all of a sudden, but I never heard why."

Mom sniffed. "That's because your father and I felt you were too young to understand at the time so we were sheltering you from the bitter truth. That man cheated on his wife, broke his family's heart, and moved them all to Seattle in disgrace. Last I heard, their oldest son was into drugs, and who knows what that girl of theirs has been up to, although if she's back in Orchard Grove and living with her aunt, I can't imagine it's good news." She shook her head. "There was something off about that family from the beginning. I told your father so the first time I met them. Too perfect to be real. Their kids were too clean, too polite, too good for it to be anything but a show." Another dramatic shake of the head, which sent her earrings jingling. "I wasn't surprised to find out what he did. Not surprised one bit. If anything, I expected it to happen sooner. He was behind the pulpit here for three or four years."

"I don't remember any of that. That's pretty sad," Ricky said.

"What's sad is that we didn't see him for what he was, at least not soon enough for it to make a difference. The church nearly shut its doors. It's only by the grace and mercy of our Heavenly Savior that Orchard Grove is still standing."

Ricky was paying more attention to the road now. If you were to believe everything Mom said, Orchard Grove Bible was in danger of closing for good at least once a quarter even though the church must be nearly a hundred years old by now.

"So how was that McAllister girl?" his mom asked. "What did she look like?"

Ricky shrugged. "She looked like a girl." In fact, the barn had been so dark he couldn't have even said what color her hair was. It wasn't until then that he realized she still had his flannel shirt. He'd have to get it back before Monday when Mom did the laundry, or he'd be in big trouble for losing it.

"Is she pretty?" Mom demanded.

"Is she what?" Ricky gripped the top of the steering wheel.

"I asked, is she pretty?"

"I don't know. Maybe." What did she expect him to say?

"Well, don't get any ideas in your head, young man. Girls like that niece of Connie's never spell anything but trouble."

CHAPTER 8

She had been stupid to move out to Orchard Grove over the weekend. If she'd been thinking clearly, she would have moved in first thing Monday morning, which would give her an entire week to warm up to the idea of stepping foot through the doors of Orchard Grove Bible Church again.

How many times had she sworn to never come back here? Yet here she was, pregnant and unmarried no less, just like so many of the old busybodies here would have expected.

She's just like her father.

It can't be helped. Remember what her dad did?

Stepping through the open doors into the high-ceilinged foyer, Jillian was overcome for a moment with dizziness. Dizziness and the overwhelming desire to either throw up Connie's cinnamon rolls or run back to Seattle and face whatever horrible memories were waiting for her there.

For all her issues at home, Seattle certainly couldn't be worse than here, could it?

"Jillian McAllister? Is that really you?"

Great. And so the onslaught began, sloppy hugs from heavily perfumed women with fake smiles proclaiming how happy they were to see her back in Orchard Grove. Grotesque and probing questions about her family. *Is your father still preaching? Are your parents together, dear? How is your brother? We heard he had a small problem, and we've all been praying for him.*

Just wait until everyone found out the truth about Jillian's pregnancy. She was surprised Aunt Connie hadn't put it on the prayer chain already.

Or maybe she had.

That would probably explain at least a few of the personal comments. *You look pale, sweetie. Are you eating well? You're still such a petite little thing, aren't you?*

You look like you could still be in high school and skinny as a rail.

Jillian had never been so grateful for a church service to begin. She sat between Connie and her uncle Dennis, with Grandma Lucy in the aisle and already starting to sway before the music began.

Didn't she know there was nothing spiritual about reading the announcements?

Jillian wondered how many more pastors had come and gone between now and the time her family had been kicked out of Orchard Grove. During their first few years in Seattle, her mom would make it a point of pride to keep up with the Women's Missionary League gossip, proclaiming every six or nine months about how Pastor So-and-So just left, and making comments about how *that church* could never keep a preacher behind the pulpit.

As if it were the church's fault and not her dad's that the elders told him to leave. As if some other church would have been more forgiving of a pastor who had an affair, or maybe it was the congregation's fault for putting their pastor under so much stress that he made such a bone-headed mistake to begin with.

The first few years had been hard. Out of the hundreds of churches in Seattle, none of them were looking to hire an adulterous pastor, no matter how profusely her dad claimed his status as a repentant, reformed husband. By the time Jillian was in high school, he finally found a congregation willing to take their chances on him. When Jillian's older brother dragged the family through several years of shame from his drug addiction and dozens of failed attempts at recovery, the church had lent the McAllister family their support. Still, when Jillian finally summoned her courage to tell her parents the truth, hasty arrangements were made to send her off to Orchard Grove.

Apparently, her parents only had the energy to deal with one black sheep in the family.

Ironically, her parents' church in Seattle would be far more gracious than the gossips who attended Orchard Grove. Here, Jillian would have to suffer through all the judgmental stares, whispered comments, and painfully intrusive questions that were sure to come. But at least her parents were spared the embarrassment their pregnant daughter would cause.

Out of sight, out of mind.

She'd managed to daydream through the opening prayer and half of the first three hymns. Oh well. Of all the things she'd done in the past to make God mad at her, getting distracted in church was probably fairly low on his list.

CHAPTER 9

Ricky hurried up the steps to the church entrance and held the door open for his mother.

"I can't believe it," she huffed. "I haven't been late in over two decades."

Ricky got the feeling Mom wasn't exaggerating.

Their Sunday morning tardiness was the result of a power flicker during the night that turned off both their alarm clocks. They still could have made it on time if it weren't for his mother's tendency to take upwards of an hour until she decided she was respectable. But still she'd found multiple ways of making Ricky feel like he was at fault for their being late.

"What would your father think?" she demanded, although with his dad away on one of his many company retreats, Ricky doubted he'd care much at all. Mom was the one who made sure the family got up and ready and presentable for church each week. Dad just showed up or else scheduled work meetings when he didn't feel like going. And since Dad was the one whose courier business paid the mortgage on their home in the Heights, Mom didn't have much leverage to complain.

Ricky sighed, certain that even though the songs had already started, Mom would still work her way into the second to front pew like normal. It was stupid for him to feel self-conscious — most everybody at this church met him when he was all of five days old and attending his very first church service — but he still wished Mom would content herself with a seat in the back.

No such luck. Oh, well. It's not like he was here to impress anybody.

There was Susannah with her sister Kitty in a wheelchair in the side aisle. He gave a little smile when Kitty looked his way. Susannah acted as if she hadn't even noticed him, which could probably be explained by the fact that she was snuggled up next to her new husband and had all her attention focused on him.

Mom made a big show of slipping past the few souls inconsiderate enough to block her way to her intended space in the pew, and he followed her, making apologies that were probably too quiet to be heard over the hymns.

Jesus paid it all. All to him I owe.

Ricky could sing the song in his sleep.

He didn't dislike church, but that was probably because he simply hadn't known anything different. As a Christian, he prayed before meals, read his Bible before bed, and came to every single service every single Sunday - stomachache, toothache, or illness. It's what he did.

Sin had left a crimson stain. He washed it white as snow.

Even though he'd lived a fairly decent (albeit uneventful) life, he knew there were still sins he needed to confess. Jealousy, for one thing. Susannah had found her happily ever after, but he was still single, left to listen to Mom complain about the way *that Peters girl* would have married him if she hadn't been foolish enough to fall in love with some exotic missionary from a foreign land known as the East Coast. Ricky never bothered to mention that Susannah had taken on her husband's name, so she couldn't really be referred to as *that Peters girl* anymore.

Oh, well.

When the next song began, Mom sang loudly beside him, but Ricky tuned her out and focused on the words.

What can wash away my sin? Nothing but the blood of Jesus.

Sometimes Ricky wondered when he'd start feeling like a Christian. He asked Jesus into his heart years ago at the same youth group retreat where his would-be girlfriend Susannah felt God call her to a future in missions, but not a whole lot had changed since then.

Maybe the spiritual life wasn't that much about how you felt but how you behaved, whether or not you were acting like the *righteous, godly* man Mom always talked about. But somewhere in the back of his head was the nagging suspicion that there was more to this whole church thing than pretending to be some upstanding gentleman with the morals and mannerisms from a century or two earlier.

The only problem was he didn't know what.

What can make me whole again? Nothing but the blood of Jesus.

Ricky resisted the urge to glance back at Susannah. She'd always been out of his league. He knew that even before she met Mr. Missionary Massachusetts Dude. But his mom had spent so many years when Ricky was a teen talking about how good of a match they'd make that he was still somewhat thrown off balance by her recent marriage.

So instead of thinking about her, he turned off his brain, sang the words that mechanically came out of his mouth, and waited for the pastor to come up and signal that it was time for everyone to sit down.

CHAPTER 10

One thing Jillian could say in defense of a church like Orchard Grove was they knew how to close a service on time. Good thing, considering how uncomfortable these pews were.

The preacher was just about to dismiss everyone when Grandma Lucy stood up.

"Pastor Greg?"

Oh no. Does she still do this?

Jillian wanted to disappear into the back of her seat.

At first the pastor acted like he hadn't heard Grandma. Smart man.

"Pastor Greg?" she repeated, and he turned with a smile Jillian would swear was forced while her grandmother asked, "May I close in prayer today?"

Greg glanced at his wristwatch. Jillian didn't know how long this particular preacher had worked at Orchard Grove, but he had apparently learned all about Grandma Lucy's delays. How could a woman that tiny and old and generally soft-spoken hold up an entire service for fifteen or twenty minutes?

And why did the pastors here always let her?

Greg let out a hefty sigh then handed her the mic. "Sure, Grandma Lucy. That'd be a real blessing."

So he was a pushover and a liar, too. Great combination for a preacher.

"Thank you." Grandma Lucy stepped into the aisle and faced the congregation. Jillian wished she'd chosen a pew closer to the back of the church. She certainly didn't want to be associated with her grandmother when she phased into one of her infamous Holy Spirit trances.

"The Lord is so good," Grandma Lucy began.

Jillian slunk a little farther in her seat. May as well try to get comfortable while she was down there. This would take a while.

"I'm so filled with awe at what the Lord's done for me, at the way he sent his Son to die on the cross to take the punishment for my sins."

Wasn't this exactly what they'd sung about eight times over this morning and then sat and listened to for the past forty-five minutes? Why did Grandma feel the compulsion to repeat everything that had just been preached?

"When I think about the sins of my past, how hardened my heart was against the Lord, I'm simply amazed at the way he chose to save a wretch like me."

As if Grandma Lucy had entertained even so much as a single sinful thought in the past half a century.

"God tells us in the book of 1 John that *if we confess our sins, he is faithful and just and will forgive us our sins and purify us from all unrighteousness.* That promise is for all of us, my friends, a promise of true forgiveness when we turn our mistakes over to the good Lord who takes our stains and makes them as white as snow."

Funny how white had become such a symbol of purity and cleanliness. From all the way back in Bible times until now, the cultural symbolism ran as strong as ever. In fact, the day Jillian told her parents she was pregnant, the very first words out of her mother's mouth were, "And you would have looked so beautiful in a white wedding dress."

Of all the things to be upset about when you find out your daughter's pregnant.

"Back in my younger days, I was lost."

It was funny to hear Grandma Lucy talk about her younger days as if they'd just been a few weeks ago. Even in the family photos that showed Jillian as a baby, Grandma Lucy was the exact same white-haired, spectacled old lady that stood now addressing a church full of adults half her age and nearly all twice her size. Jillian was no bodybuilder, but she was certain she could lift Grandma Lucy off the ground with one hand if she ever found a reason to.

"I thought I knew the Lord," Grandma Lucy said, "but I was still living by the set of rules others had told me made up the Christian life. I was still acting as if I could earn my way into God's grace by the good things I did. Even as a young woman on the mission field, I didn't fully know God for who he was until he opened my eyes. Let me see how wretched I truly was. And that's when I learned to depend on him. That's when my walk with Christ started."

Jillian had heard it all before. Grandma Lucy recited her conversion story every Christmas, Thanksgiving, and any other major holiday that saw more than two or three relatives together under the same roof. Out of her dozens of cousins, Jillian figured each and every one of them (including those whose names she couldn't even remember) had memorized Grandma Lucy's testimony word for word.

It was great that Grandma Lucy was so steadfast in her walk with Christ. And if it hadn't been for the way that this very church turned their backs on Jillian's family — as if she and her brother and mom were just as much to blame for her father's adultery as he was — maybe she'd be as fiery for God as her grandmother was. She knew that's what Grandma Lucy hoped as she rocked the hours away in her prayer chair.

Oh, well. Grandma Lucy was just another one of those people Jillian would end up disappointing.

CHAPTER 11

Ricky leaned forward in his seat. His palms were sweaty, and his leg jiggled so fast his mom put her hand on his knee and squeezed hard.

He couldn't stop.

"We serve a God of power, glory, and incredible, infinite might."

He'd heard Grandma Lucy preach like this scores of times, but for some reason today her words reached out and grabbed hold of him. He couldn't resist even if he wanted to.

Which he didn't.

"In spite of his unspeakable majesty and strength, in spite of his immeasurable greatness, this same God has called you his own. This same God who set the stars and the heavens into place knows your name, knows your fears and sorrows and your secret inmost longings. The psalmist says he's intimately familiar with all your ways. You're beloved of the Most High God. So what is there on earth to make you afraid?"

How could it be that this little old spitfire was saying truths he'd known his entire life, but today they made his heart race as if he were hearing them for the very first time?

She looked at him, and something zipped through his heart like electricity. A surge of power. A desire to understand this God she worshipped, to really, fully know him.

"The Lord will raise you up on eagle's wings and carry your sanctification on to completion."

She was using all the same words, all the same phrases he'd heard in church his entire life. Why did they suddenly have such intensity behind them? Why did he feel as if she were peering into his soul?

"Calm down," his mom snapped and pinched his bouncing knee.

He hardly noticed.

This was the answer he'd been looking for. This was what it meant to live out a godly, righteous life. Not holding doors open for little old ladies or being punctual or always coming to church with a clean and pressed shirt. This God who created the stars and held them all in place in the universe — what did he care about starched collars or straight neckties?

"Today I want to do something a little unorthodox," Grandma Lucy declared.

Mom sniffed in her seat, but for once, Ricky didn't care what she thought. Her version of righteous living was so different from the glimpse he'd just seen that he wondered if she really knew anything about God or the Bible or the way to true satisfaction in Christ.

"I want anyone who's longing for more of God to come forward. I know we don't do altar calls nearly as much as we used to back in the olden days, but God's putting it on my heart that there's someone here. Someone who needs to hear and respond to his invitation for a fuller, more satisfied life. Someone who has lived knowing about God, but now it's time for them to really know God in all his power and matchless love. If that sounds like you today, I want you to come forward so I can pray with you."

Ricky hesitated for a single moment, the same moment when Mom's hand gripped his knee even more tightly.

Ignoring her pointed glare and the heat of her disapproving anger, he stood up and walked forward on eager, steady legs straight toward Grandma Lucy.

CHAPTER 12

Jillian couldn't remember a longer service. As humiliated as she was for Grandma Lucy making such a scene at the end, outshining the pastor and leading the congregation in one of those old-fashioned, emotionally laden altar calls, she was even more relieved when it was finally over.

Connie was busy talking to some friends, Uncle Dennis was waiting by the door holding Connie's purse, and Grandma Lucy was still up front, praying for that gangly boy who'd been the only one to walk up the aisle.

After all the charisma she'd thrown into that emotional appeal, Grandma Lucy only got one customer willing to risk his own personal dignity and come to the front for prayer.

How embarrassing.

Jillian would never make a fool out of herself like that. What was so wrong with maintaining your walk with God and your commitment to him in the quietness and privacy of your own heart?

Did her grandmother think they were back in the days of big-tent revivals and old-fashioned gospel meetings?

Oh, well. It was finally over and they could go back to the farmhouse. At least they could once Connie was done chattering away and Grandma Lucy finished praying with that boy.

Poor kid. You'd have to be some kind of desperate to walk in front of everybody and let a little old lady pray over you like that.

Jillian wouldn't be caught dead doing the same.

The one good thing that came out of Grandma Lucy's whole impromptu revival call was that the congregants were mostly all eager to head home. No more awkward conversations like before the service. Everybody in Orchard Grove, at least the older generations, treated punctuality as the most prized of virtues, and nobody wanted to be late for lunch.

Come to think of it, neither did she.

"Hey, there, Jillian. How you doing today?"

She glanced up at the tall boy who'd been praying with her grandmother just a few moments earlier.

"It's me."

"Okay." Was that supposed to mean something? He looked slightly familiar, but that was probably because he was the only individual in the entire church desperate enough to risk his own personal embarrassment and walk to the front of the sanctuary.

"Hey, you gonna be home later this afternoon? I might have to swing by and pick up my flannel."

His flannel? Did he think she was somebody else?

"You don't need to wash it or anything. My mom will take care of that Monday."

Lovely. A mama's boy. Just the kind of guy she wanted hanging around. Now if she could only figure out why he was talking as if he knew her.

"Hey, how'd the milking go today?" He offered a cocky grin that looked more like a grimace than anything else. "Hope you didn't spill any buckets today."

Oh, yeah. HIM.

"I think I left your shirt in the barn. You can just swing by and pick it up whenever you want."

His expression fell. Had she said something rude?

"Okay. Well, maybe I'll do that. Does three o'clock sound like a good time?"

She shrugged. "Whatever."

"Great. I'll see you then. Or, I mean, I'll see my shirt

then. In the barn you said, right?"

"Yup."

"Cool. Well, I'll drop by and pick it up."

"Okay." Had they seriously spent this long talking about nothing more than a dirty flannel?

"So, three. Right? You'll be home?"

Another shrug. "Even if we're not, the barn's always open."

"Right. The barn. You said the shirt's in the barn."

She nodded.

"Great. That's awesome. No, that's really cool."

Swell, she thought to herself and came up with a few more fitting adjectives she could lend him if he ran out.

"Well, see you later. I mean, if you're there at three. In the barn."

She turned away before he could see her roll her eyes. At the same time, some woman hustled up and grabbed him by the arm and hissed into his ear. Jillian didn't hear it all but caught enough to make out *with that girl*, and then they were gone.

Jillian watched them leave, figuring with a mother like that it'd make sense for anyone to run up a church aisle just to get away from her for a few seconds.

Studying her fingernails, she waited, counting down the

minutes until her aunt finished yakking with her friends and they could all go home and get something to eat.

CHAPTER 13

"Have another helping." Connie heaped more stew into Jillian's bowl. "We certainly don't want you going hungry. Not when you're eating for two."

Uncle Dennis had already retreated into his den to read his newspaper. It was only her aunt and her grandmother with her at the table. She'd known both women since she was a baby, so why did she feel so awkward?

Grandma Lucy didn't have much to say. Apparently, she'd used up her quota of words preaching at all the members of Orchard Grove Bible Church. Didn't she know how rude it was to take up everyone's time, make them all late …

Thank God for crockpot meals. Jillian didn't think she could have waited even ten more minutes before getting something into her system. She'd spent nearly the entire first trimester queasy. Now, her body was making up for lost calories. She'd need a third helping of stew before she could say she was fully satisfied. Of course, the itty-bitty glass bowls Connie served it in were partially to blame.

"So, dear, what do you have planned for the week?" Connie asked.

Jillian stared and blinked once or twice. What did she have planned? Did her aunt seriously think she came to Orchard Grove with some sort of itinerary?

"Remind me to call the clinic and make you an appointment when they open tomorrow. Your mom says you haven't been to the doctor yet."

No, she hadn't. Just a long chat with the nurse at the center in Seattle where she'd gotten her free pregnancy test. Some pee on a stick, four minutes of waiting, that thin pink line, and her life was put on hold.

What kind of parent kicks their adult daughter out of the house just for getting knocked up? Didn't her mom and dad realize how easily she could have gone and aborted her baby, and they could have kept up their appearances as a godly, righteous family? Who in the twenty-first century sends their daughter to live with her aunt until her baby's born? It was like a plot from a century-and-a-half-old novel they'd make a bunch of unwilling high-schoolers read in English lit class.

Only this was Jillian's life and not some piece of

fiction.

But what could she do? She'd already resigned herself to six months of exile. Then she'd put the baby up for adoption, move back to Seattle, and get on with life as usual. Most of the people at church thought she'd hauled herself out here to help take care of her grandmother, who'd suffered some health concerns last winter.

The hardest part was not knowing how many people knew. It might just be her parents, that crisis pregnancy nurse, and her extended family at Safe Anchorage.

Or it might be half the congregation in Seattle and the entire congregation (and thus by extension the entire town) of Orchard Grove.

"Isn't it a little early to need to see a doctor?" she asked. In what was probably not the wisest of choices, she'd avoided any research about pregnancy except for a couple pamphlets she picked up at the center. Call it denial or something else, but she still didn't feel like she needed to see a doctor. Not yet. Her belly was hardly swollen, and she hadn't felt the baby move at all.

If it weren't for her sluggish appetite the past three months and that little pink line she saw in the pregnancy center counseling room, she'd have a hard time believing there was a real child in there at all.

Maybe it was a mistake.

Then she could go back home. Finish her classes …

The more she thought about all she was missing, the angrier she got. What kind of parent would rather hide a pregnancy than see their daughter succeed in school?

It shouldn't surprise her, though. The McAllister family was all about keeping up appearances.

Keeping up appearances when her dad had the audacity to have that affair.

Keeping up appearances whenever they went interviewing at churches around Seattle.

Keeping up appearances when her brother was in rehab, and she was schooled and drilled and trained to only give the vaguest of replies when people asked where he was or how he was doing.

And now it was all about keeping up appearances so her parents wouldn't suffer the embarrassment of having two children who turned out to be spiritual failures instead of just one.

Jillian had thought things were tough when the folks at Orchard Grove kicked her dad out from behind the pulpit. But then her friends weren't even allowed to play with her anymore. As if the sinful McAllister influence might stain their children and ruin their innocence.

She'd been young when it happened, but not too young to understand they were being treated unfairly, especially her mother, who was most to be pitied out of everyone involved. Instead of surrounding her and showing their love and support, women her mom had considered her closest friends snubbed her, treated her as if she were some sort of spiritual pariah for daring to marry a man who claimed to be a preacher yet would go out and cheat on his wife.

That's why Jillian had sworn so many times to never set foot in that church again, except here she was, and now she was the outcast. Or she would be once the truth came out. The pastor's kid with an illegitimate child. If these short-sighted gossips knew a fraction of what she'd gone through …

But it didn't matter. Explaining her side of the story wouldn't change a thing. She just had to ride out the next six months, make arrangements to find an adoptive family to take her child in, and then life could go back to normal.

Hopefully at least.

CHAPTER 14

"I still don't understand what gave you the compulsion to stand up and walk in front of everybody like some kind of lunatic." Mom had opened her mouth in the church parking lot and hadn't shut it yet twenty minutes later after they made their way to the restaurant at the Main Street Hotel, found their seats, and waited for their drinks to come.

She leaned forward, trying to keep her voice low since part of being a *righteous and godly woman* meant never expressing your frustrations or anger in public. "Did you stop and think what type of message you were sending everyone else about our family?"

"No. I wasn't thinking about any of that. I already told you." The longer his mother talked, the more Ricky realized that she'd never experienced God's presence or power the way he had during Grandma Lucy's closing words. If she had, she'd be congratulating him instead of lecturing him about how his actions may have projected badly on their family.

"What will people say? Now everyone will think I raised you godless. That you didn't know the Lord until some crazy old woman stands up and says a few words into a microphone. Tell me. What did that woman say that your Sunday school teachers or I haven't been teaching you for years?"

"Nothing. It's just that … Something felt different this time."

She let out a huff. "Felt different. And what exactly do you think will happen if anyone who gets any sort of inkling or urge to get closer to God just decides to stand right up and say a prayer right there in front of everybody? Do you know what people will say?"

Ricky stared at his menu. Mom could rail all she wanted, but he knew he'd done the right thing. The mature thing.

The first major decision in his adult life that hadn't been made for him.

And it felt good.

"You know what?" He hesitated for just a moment. After all, this was her celebration lunch. If he ruined the mood, she'd make sure he heard about it for weeks to come.

This time, it was a chance he was willing to take.

"You know what?" he repeated. "If you want my opinion, this whole town cares far too much about everyone else's business. What's that Jesus says about removing the speck of dust from someone else's eye when you have a plank stuck in your own?"

Mom crossed her arms. "Oh. So now that you and Grandma Lucy are so close, you feel that gives you the right to start reciting Scripture to your mother who taught you how to read the Bible in the first place? Is that it, Big Britches? You know, I told your father there was a rebellious streak in you. I did, and he said I was overreacting, but I told him time and time again, *That son of yours is going to cause us problems one day. You mark my words.* Well." She clapped her hands together, apparently forgetting her own advice on how demure little church women are supposed to act.

"Well," she repeated in a more subdued tone, "you might think you're a big man now, but I'll tell you what. Any fool can walk in front of the church and have a little old lady pray for him. And what do you think? That your father and I don't pray for you already? What's wrong with our prayers, I'd like to know. Don't you think they count?"

He raised his eyebrows, startled both by the intensity of his mom's outburst and his own refusal to cower before her. "You do know that me going up that aisle has nothing to do with you, right?"

She scoffed again. "Don't deceive yourself. It has everything to do with me, and you and I both know it. You think I did a poor job raising you, that my prayers for you aren't as special because I'm not some Holy Ghost fanatic like that Grandma Lucy. Like her silly little spectacles or those gaudy blouses she always wears somehow make her holier than the rest of us."

"Wait," Ricky interrupted. "What in the world do her blouses have to do with anything?"

"Apparently a whole lot, because that's the only reason I can come up with for why you would throw away every shred of dignity your father and I have tried to instill in you since the day you were born. You come from a long line of respectable men and women, and you're expected to carry on the family name as well as the family legacy, which includes hard work and a righteous and godly lifestyle. Not leaping down a church aisle like you're some sort of teenager at a co-ed dance."

He wondered if his mom had even attended one of these

so-called *co-ed dances*, but he knew enough to keep his mouth shut.

"All I'm saying," she finally concluded, "is I want you to remember that you're not just representing your father and me and the family business. You're representing all four of your grandparents and everyone who came before them too. And I can't begin to tell you how many of your ancestors would be rolling in their graves if they were around to see the scene you made at church today. A scene I trust you'll be wise enough in the future to never repeat. Right?"

"What?" Ricky had stopped listening. He was too busy trying to figure out where this spiritual fire in his soul had come from, wondering how his life had ever felt even close to complete without it and running through everything he knew about God and church and the Bible to find a way to make sure the feeling never left him now that he'd finally grabbed hold of it.

CHAPTER 15

"And this is our cash register, but you'll have to wait until the store opens up again tomorrow morning so I can show you how to work it," Connie prattled.

The stench of scented candles and lotions was so strong that Jillian wondered how anyone could step foot in this gift shop without puking, let alone work here for an entire day.

"And back here," Connie continued, "is where we keep the inventory. Dennis handles all that, so you won't have to worry, but when it comes time to stock the shelves, I'll show you how to make it look nice and tidy. I don't trust my husband on that side of it. No eye for beauty at all, that man. But I'm sure you're going to do just fine. Did I go too fast? Do you need me to repeat anything?"

"I'm sure it will be fine," Jillian assured her. Just how difficult did her aunt think a single shift in the gift shop would be? Hopefully, it would give Jillian something to do to get her mind off her situation. If anything, she was worried that tomorrow morning would find her bored out of her mind behind the counter half an hour after opening.

"Of course," Connie went on, "I'll be around all day so if you run into any problems, you just need to holler. I was telling Dennis, now that we have you here to help, I can finally get working on that wedding album for your uncle Joseph and aunt Jolene. Wasn't that a lovely ceremony?"

Jillian was hardly listening. It was partially cute and partially pathetic how big a deal Connie was making out of this simple job standing behind the counter and running a few credit cards a day. Jillian had worked retail before in Seattle's busiest mall. The only thing she was really worried about was growing too bored. "Do you have WiFi here?"

"Why what?"

Jillian hoped her aunt didn't see the way she rolled her eyes. What century did these people think they were in? "WiFi," she repeated. "For the Internet."

Connie puckered her lips into a pout. "What are you needing that for now? You know your uncle and I don't agree with that online dating so many young folks have taken up with these days. Even one of the girls from our own church, sweetest thing you'd ever meet ..."

"I'm not looking for someone to date," Jillian interrupted. "I just want to check email, see what my friends have posted."

"Posted?"

Jillian shook her head. "Never mind. I'll just use the signal from my phone."

Great. While she was banished to the desert areas of Orchard Grove, the armpit of Washington state if there ever was one, Jillian would give her parents yet another reason to be disappointed in her when they saw how much data she was using up in their shared plan.

Oh, well. That's what happens when you put family appearances above all else.

She was so sick of it. Up until the move itself, she'd been more worried about the pregnancy, about taking time off her studies and missing out on the social life she'd worked so hard to build. But now that she was here, she had nothing better to do but stew over how unfairly her parents were treating her.

Being in Orchard Grove itself didn't help matters either. She'd tried so hard to forget this town, forget the church and how deplorably they treated her in the past. It wasn't until she was forced to sit through an entire sermon after being bombarded by nosy questions from congregants who had shunned her and her family so many years ago that she realized how much bitterness she was still holding onto.

It's one thing to fire a pastor who does something as stupid as her dad did. She had no problem with that. But why would the church turn and make her mom feel as if she were just as much to blame? Why would all those oh-so-proper mothers forbid their children to play with Jillian and her brother anymore? Did they think that lust was hereditary? Well, how did they think the human race had sustained itself through the millennia?

Back in Seattle, with the busyness of her college courses and a full social schedule, she didn't spare Orchard Grove a fleeting thought. But that was impossible now she was stuck here for six full months, reminded every single day of the church that had forced her to turn her back on God in the first place.

If it hadn't been for the way she and her family had been treated, Jillian probably would have continued on leading that little Sunday school life everyone expected of her. Hadn't she been trained since the time she was a toddler to act like a proper pastor's kid? Then her dad got himself kicked out from the ministry, and Jillian realized that all those people her family had tried so hard to impress weren't even worth the oxygen they breathed.

What else is there to say about a group of so-called Christians who would make a little girl feel like she was shameful and unclean just because her daddy did a Very Bad Thing?

Sure, she had made some stupid choices herself since then, but didn't the root of it all point back here?

"Well, now," Connie declared, "I've got some bread rising that I need to check on, and then after dinner I'll show you how we put the kids down for the night."

It took Jillian a few seconds to realize her aunt was talking about the goats.

Connie grabbed the keys to the store and turned off the lights. "You don't know what an answer to prayer this is for me. I was telling your uncle just today how much I've been praying for a little help around the store."

Jillian accepted her aunt's hug stiffly.

"I'm so very excited to have you with us here," Connie sighed.

That makes one of us, Jillian thought to herself.

CHAPTER 16

"Come on, Peaches," Jillian pleaded. "Just get in here so I can tuck you in for the night."

There she went again, talking to these animals as if they were tiny human beings. Connie had run back to the house to pull some bread out of the oven. They had managed to get everyone into the pen, all except for Peaches, who wouldn't come near no matter how much grain Jillian held out to coax her indoors.

"You know, I have a good mind to make you sleep outside just to teach you a lesson."

"Someone throwing a temper tantrum before bed?"

The voice made her jump. She whipped her head around, nearly banging her shoulder on the barn door.

"Here. Let me help." Ricky held his empty hand out toward the goat and made the same sort of *tsk tsk tsk* you'd use to call a cat. Surprisingly enough, Peaches let him get close enough to grab her by the bright collar clasped around her neck. "You naughty little thing," Ricky crooned to her. "Don't you know it's time for bed?"

He held the opening just wide enough for Peaches to pass through and gave her a few friendly pats on the rump before closing the barn door and latching it shut.

"Thanks." Jillian was so tired from the entire ordeal of getting the animals to bed that she didn't have the energy to say anything else.

"It's no problem. Peaches and I go way back. I actually helped deliver her."

Jillian was certain that somewhere behind the words was at least a partially interesting story, but her back was aching, her stomach still grumbling after that heavy clam chowder for dinner, and her whole body was exhausted. If there was a tale, she'd listen to it some other time.

"It happened when I was out here helping Dennis with the milking because Connie was out of town at the women's retreat, and ..."

"Did you find your shirt?" Jillian interrupted.

"My what?"

"Your shirt. Isn't that what you came here for?"

"Oh. That." He looked around as if his flannel might magically appear. "I was by here already. I came at three.

Didn't I tell you that?" He shifted from one foot to the other. "I came by and picked it up after I took my mom out for lunch. Didn't you see me? I waved."

When would she have seen him? "I was in my room all afternoon."

"I know. I saw you in the window. You were staring right at me, and I waved and held up my shirt so you'd know I got it."

She shrugged.

"You didn't see me?"

"Guess not." Or if she had, he'd been so nondescript she hadn't paid him any attention and had already forgotten the exchange.

"Well, I got my shirt earlier. At three, like I said."

"So what are you doing here now?"

"I just came because Connie wanted to borrow some brewer's yeast, except my mom's not feeling too well. She's got this thing going on in her hip. Sciatic nerve pain. Makes it hard for her to get up and down, so I told her I'd drive it over. That's what I do for a living, you know. I'm a driver for my dad's courier business."

"Good for you."

"Yeah." He smiled. "Thanks. It's a pretty good job."

"I bet." Could he tell she was done with this

conversation? In fact, she'd been done as soon as he got Peaches inside for her. "Thanks for helping with the goats," she said, hoping he'd take that as his cue to leave.

Unfortunately, he stayed exactly where he was. "Oh, don't mention it. Peaches can be stubborn, but she's such a sweet little thing once you get to know her."

I'll bet she is, Jillian thought.

"Well, I guess I better go." He sounded so disappointed. As if they'd been having some kind of great heart to heart.

"All right. See you later."

"Yeah." He shifted from one foot to the other again, scratched his cheek and next his chin, and then turned around.

Jillian sighed and started back to the house. She'd only been in Orchard Grove for the weekend, and she already regretted she ever came.

CHAPTER 17

Ricky walked slowly back to the car. Something had been nagging him since he saw Jillian outside struggling with that barn door.

She was lonely. And who could blame her? After all her family had gone through when her dad was the pastor here, why would she want to come back?

He'd heard his mom on the phone with several of her friends from the Women's Missionary League this afternoon. Everyone was speculating on what might have compelled *that McAllister girl* to return to Orchard Grove. The public explanation was she'd come to help take care of her grandmother, but other than a short hospital stay last December, Grandma Lucy was in perfectly fine health.

So the rest was a whole lot of conjecture that would have made Ricky embarrassed for Jillian even if they'd never met before.

He glanced back at Jillian, who was making her way to the house. She didn't seem to remember too much about him, but he remembered her. She and her brother were always well-dressed and well-behaved. He heard it so often from Mom, he could never forget. *Why can't you sit still in church? You don't see Pastor Joel's son bouncing his leg up and down, do you?*

Or *your teacher told me that Jillian's the only one who prays out loud in Sunday school. Why don't you ever volunteer? A godly and righteous boy should be willing to pray whenever the teacher needs somebody.*

Back then, he figured Jillian and her brother were as stuck-up and uninteresting as his mother made them out to be. But things changed after her dad got kicked out from behind the pulpit. Last he heard, Jillian's brother was in rehab with some sort of a drug problem, and Jillian was no longer the soft-spoken, demure little thing she'd been as a girl with her curly hair and poofy dresses.

What happened to her?

He couldn't blame her if she was mad at Orchard Grove for the way they'd treated her family. Even though his mom didn't tell him the full extent of Pastor Joel's indiscretions, he understood even as a kid that the McAllister family devolved from being a model of righteous, godly living to spiritual outcasts. The change happened overnight. Mom wouldn't explain the details, but she made it clear he wasn't supposed to speak to either of the McAllister kids again. Ever.

He shook his head. He'd been growing tired of his mother's constant henpecking for quite a while now, but he'd put up with it because deep in his heart, he really did like the sound of being a *righteous and godly man*. But something had changed in him, not just after the church service when he prayed with Grandma Lucy but after his lunch with Mom afterwards.

What kind of mother chides her son for pursuing a relationship with God? What kind of woman emphasizes *righteous and godly appearances* over actual obedience or an intimate knowledge of the Lord?

While he'd been praying with Grandma Lucy, he'd surrendered himself to God's will. Told the Lord he'd do anything he wanted him to. Head to the mission field, become a pastor — wherever God led him, he was prepared to follow. He had no idea at the time that God would ask him to live with his mother's pointed disapproval. In retrospect, moving to Africa and starting up a Christian orphanage or preaching to heathens in the Amazon jungle felt like easier callings.

But he could do it. Even over lunch, he was surprised at the fearlessness he felt. Strange as it might sound, today might have been the first time he realized his mother had just as many faults as anyone else, which was saying a lot, given how she set herself up to be the epitome of that righteous and godly lifestyle she so vehemently preached.

I don't have to be afraid of disappointing her. She's just a person. It was a realization he should have come to years ago. He'd never considered himself a strong or brave or bold man. In fact, his mother had taught him from the earliest age that a righteous and godly boy would never think of talking back or second guessing his parents.

But he was an adult now, and it was time for him to take control of his own life and his own destiny, whether or not Mom approved of his decisions. Maybe she'd tease him for wanting to grow in his faith. Maybe she'd get jealous if he put his walk with God before his relationship with her, but he wasn't accountable to her anymore.

He didn't have to be the kind of Christian she was. The kind who would shun a friend whose husband made a mistake. The kind who would spread hurtful gossip guised as prayer requests about a girl like Jillian.

He wasn't going to be that kind of believer. And if Mom didn't like it, that was her problem and not his.

The idea was as novel as it was freeing.

He didn't have to be afraid of disappointing anyone but God.

Halfway to his car, he spun around on his heels. "Jillian! Jillian! Wait!"

He was sprinting now. He had to hurry if he wanted to catch her before she disappeared into the house.

He tripped once but regained his balance before nearly plowing into her on the porch.

"What is it?"

He could tell by her tone she wasn't happy he'd come back.

That was okay, too.

Jillian was like him. She'd been hurt by the same set of unyielding, unforgiving rules that listed out a thousand different ways to be righteous and godly, none of which had anything to do with a real and personal relationship with the Lord.

If he could make her see things the way he did now, maybe it could break through that hardened, angry exterior.

It was worth a try.

"What do you want?" she demanded again.

He started to stammer but reminded himself he was a new man. The kind of man who wasn't afraid to do the right thing. To extend his friendship to Jillian, who might not find another compassionate soul in this entire town.

"I was just wondering if maybe you wanted to hang out." As soon as the words left his mouth, he realized he'd made a mistake. He didn't want her to think this was a date. "Not like, you know, I'm not asking you for *that* or anything. I just … I was only thinking … Maybe we could eat something …"

Eat something? What was he talking about?

"I'm pretty busy this week, but thanks."

She turned around, and before Ricky could recover his breath from running so hard and fumbling so pathetically over his words, she was inside the house, and he was staring at the shut door.

CHAPTER 18

He couldn't believe it. How could he be so awkward? The fact that Jillian turned him down wasn't as embarrassing as the realization that she thought he'd been asking her out on a date to begin with. It was nothing like that. Not even close. To think that she would go on believing he was interested in her romantically was even more humiliating than getting rejected in the first place.

He was so distraught he wasn't even in the mood to listen to the oldies station in the car. He had to find a way to make it right, to explain himself better. But how?

Hey there, Jillian. Remember that night when you thought I was asking you out on a date, and you slammed the door in my face? Really, I just wanted to spend a little time with you because out of everybody here in Orchard Grove, I thought that maybe you were lonely enough that you needed a friend. So I felt sorry for you and that's why I offered to spend some time together.

It would never work.

The drive back from Safe Anchorage Farm to his family's house on the Heights gave him time to calm down a little bit. At least he'd tried. He needed to be careful. This new religious excitement of his would keep on getting him in trouble if he didn't learn how to tone it down every now and then.

Even though he'd had an unforgettable experience today at church, he was still the same old Ricky Fields — clumsy, awkward, more afraid to stand up for himself than not, and woefully unable to communicate clearly with members of the opposite gender, which is what caused him so much trouble with Jillian in the first place.

He didn't even want to imagine how pathetic she must think he was.

Oh, well. There wasn't anything he could do about it.

He pulled into his family's cul-de-sac. His mom had been giddy with excitement when they finally had enough money to move to Orchard Grove Heights. Ricky still couldn't see what the big deal was. It took longer to get here than anywhere else in town, and the hillside was infamously icy in the winter. But his mom's version of a righteous and godly husband was someone who could afford the mortgage on a place like this, and his dad had finally delivered.

Tomorrow Ricky would start a regular work week driving for his dad's company, so he might as well head to bed early and let his wounded ego recover.

If he was lucky, Mom would be on the phone or in the bedroom, watching one of those sappy romances she loved so much.

He opened the door and stepped into the house.

He was not lucky.

"Ricky, your father and I want to talk to you."

It was rare to see the two of them voluntarily in the same room unless it was a holiday or they were entertaining work colleagues. Ricky was instantly on the defensive. "If this is about church ..."

His mother let out a forced laugh. "It has nothing to do with today, son. Sit down. We want to talk to you."

What choice did he have? He pulled out a chair, bumping his elbow on the table and nearly smashing his foot under one of the legs before he managed to sit down and face his parents.

Mom primped her hair. "We know you haven't had too much luck in the dating world, and so your father and I have decided it's time to help you out a little bit."

Immediately Ricky wished for a dozen lectures about

the way he'd stood up today and walked down the aisle. Anything would be better than this.

He glanced at his father, whose gaze was focused on a pile of magazines on the coffee table between them.

"I know you're a shy boy, but that doesn't mean you can't find a nice, godly girl to date. But seeing as how you'd never find the courage to ask the right one out if you met her, your father and I decided it was time for us to be a little bit more proactive on your behalf."

Proactive? He felt almost as nervous as he had three years ago when he sat in the doctor's office with his mom to find out the results of her cancer screening.

"One of the problems, aside from your being so shy like we've already said, is that Orchard Grove is an aging community. We figured that if we wanted to broaden your chances of meeting the right girl, we'd have to look at some outside sources."

Ricky's leg was bouncing so fast his mom finally picked up one of the magazines on the coffee table and slapped him with it.

"Stop fidgeting like that. It isn't godly to be so nervous. Now listen. We set you up with a profile on that Soulmates website, and there's a very nice young woman who's going to meet you Tuesday night at the Olive Garden in

Wenatchee."

"What?"

"Don't worry. I'll show you all the messages so you can get a feel for what she already knows about you. I think you're really going to like her. Her name is Carly, and she's got strawberry blonde hair and a cute little dimple and she ..."

"And she's willing to date me after exchanging emails with my mother?"

Mom waved her hand in the air. "She didn't know it was me. She thinks she's been talking to you."

Ricky stood up. This was ridiculous. "It's one thing to meddle, but it's even worse to pretend to be someone else and risk hurting an innocent stranger."

Mom reached out for his hand. "Don't you think you're overreacting?" She smacked Dad in the side, and he looked up from his magazine.

"What?"

"Tell your son that he's overreacting. Mothers like me have been setting their little boys up for centuries. Tell him."

Dad shrugged and mumbled, "It does seem a little weird if you ask me."

"What do you know anyway?" Mom huffed. She shook

her head, straightened her spine, and stared at Ricky. "Now be a good boy and go upstairs. I emailed you your login information and everything else so you can learn all about Carly. I found a real winner, you know. You're really going to like her."

He didn't stick around to argue anymore. At least if he were able to communicate directly with this Carly girl, he could explain to her that it was all just one big mistake and move on with his life.

Without trusting his voice to say another word, he went upstairs to his room and turned on his computer.

CHAPTER 19

Jillian laughed every time she thought about it. That gangly, awkward farm boy actually had a crush on her?

Orchard Grove was admittedly a small town, but surely somewhere was a girl better suited for someone like Ricky — most likely a shy, awkward, homely type.

It was so humorous that she wasn't even insulted by him thinking he might actually stand a chance with her.

All the goats were put away in the barn. Grandma Lucy was asleep while Connie and Dennis had retired early to their bedroom, Jillian found herself alone for nearly the first time since she arrived in Orchard Grove.

She pulled out her phone to check for any messages, trying to come up with a few clever adages that would describe just how ridiculous it was to be trapped in a backwards town like this.

She refreshed her phone twice. No notifications from

anybody?

She let out a sigh. *Well, that's life for you.*

What she needed was a new crowd. Not like that Ricky boy with his clumsy ways and awkward words. Where did young people go to have fun all the way out here? Maybe Wenatchee? It was the only nearby city she could think of with more than a few thousand people. She typed it into her browser.

Meet singles in Wenatchee. The pop up with the photo of laughing, smiling friends — the kind of friends she left behind in Seattle — caught her eye. *Free fourteen-day trial.*

She shrugged. She'd never tried Internet dating in Seattle because her social calendar was always full. She entered in the login information to start a new account then browsed through the selfies on her phone until she found a suitable profile picture.

An error screen popped up. *Profile pictures for paid users only. Click here to upgrade.*

Great. Her wallet was somewhere, but she didn't feel like digging it out. For now, she'd just rely on their stupid little cartoon avatar and upgrade later.

The app took her through a few preliminary questions, and in five minutes she had created her personal page.

CHAPTER 20

Ricky couldn't believe that he had to drive all the way out to Wenatchee just to tell some girl he'd never met that the man she agreed to date turned out to be a middle-aged meddling mother.

He had tried to contact Carly all week, but her inbox at Soulmates was full. The last note Mom received said how excited she was to meet him at Olive Garden and that she'd be there wearing a teal turtleneck sweater.

He would never admit it to anybody, but he had to Google teal to make sure he knew what color to look for.

An hour and a half drive just to dump somebody. And there weren't even any good oldies stations once he got out of Orchard Grove County.

Every once in a while he wondered what might happen if he went ahead with the date as planned, but he knew that wouldn't be fair to Carly. He had already rehearsed what he was going to say, how he was going to apologize for the way his mom had interfered, ask her to forgive them both for wasting her time, and wish her luck on finding the love of her life.

It was possible — just slightly possible — that even after he confessed everything, she would go ahead and agree to have dinner with him anyway, but part of Ricky hoped she'd storm off angrily so he could go home and prove to his mom what a tremendous mess she'd made of things.

He wondered what Carly looked like. Her account profile was one of those cartoon faces only, and all he knew from her personal page were some very basic statistics. Strawberry blonde hair. Fair skin and freckles.

Ricky glanced again at the time. Twenty or thirty minutes left at most. Half an hour before he could find this girl with the strawberry blonde hair wearing the teal turtleneck sweater and let her know that this entire date had been one huge, embarrassing mistake.

CHAPTER 21

Before he got out of his car, Ricky did one more Google search to make sure he remembered what color teal was, then he did another search for turtleneck sweaters just to be safe.

He stepped outside the car and glanced at the restaurant's exterior, wondering if Olive Garden would be any good. His mother hated to eat anywhere besides the Main Street Hotel, where she knew the owners and was convinced they weren't going to sneeze on her food or poison her drinks. He'd never been to Olive Garden before, but he'd seen commercials and had heard people raving about the breadsticks. His stomach rumbled, and he paused to wonder for just a moment if it would be ethical to wait until after their appetizers to tell Carly the full truth.

No, definitely not. Which was a pity since Ricky hadn't thought about how hungry he'd be on the drive back home from Wenatchee.

He stepped inside the door, surprised at how dim the whole place was. How could people read their menus or see the food in front of them?

"Welcome to Olive Garden. Do you have reservations?"

Ricky fumbled in his pocket to pull out a cellphone, which he dropped to the floor. On his way up from retrieving it, he banged his shoulder into the little podium where the young woman stood staring down at him.

"Reservations?" she asked again.

He thought through all his messages from Soulmates. Had Carly said anything about reservations?

"I didn't know I needed them. I'm here waiting for someone. I'm not sure either of us thought to call ahead."

The woman stared at him quizzically and then shrugged. "It will be about a twenty-minute wait. What should I put you down for?"

His mouth had grown unbelievably dry. "For now just breadsticks. Breadsticks and water. Or better make that two sodas."

"No, I just want to know what name to write down."

Ricky's face heated up. "Oh." He wiped his sweaty palms on his pants. "Oh," he repeated. "Sorry about that.

I've never eaten here before."

"So what name?"

"Oh yeah. Carly."

She stared at him again, shrugged, and scribbled something down on her tablet. "All right, Mr. Carly. Just have a seat, and we'll call you when there's a table free."

So that's why she wanted a name. Why did they have to make things so complicated here?

He glanced at the time. It was still only 4:45. He wondered how long he'd have to wait. Every time the door opened, he glanced up to see if it was a girl in a teal turtleneck sweater, but everything was so dimly lit here he realized it would be next to impossible to tell one color from another.

He decided to pass the time people-watching since there wasn't anything better for him to do. He was surprised at how many older couples there were, men and women his mom and dad's age or older. His own parents had never once gone out together in all of Ricky's working memory, and he wondered if perhaps his mom and dad were an abnormality.

He made himself a mental note to take his wife out to dinner at least once a year no matter how long they'd been married. Of course, he'd have to find a wife first for that little romantic tip to serve any practical use.

"Excuse me." Something familiar in the voice startled him, and he turned to see a young woman talking to the greeter behind her podium. "I was in the restroom and think I might have missed getting seated."

Ricky couldn't believe it. How much more awkward and embarrassing could this night get?

"Jillian?" He stood up and walked toward her. She was still wearing the windbreaker, so he couldn't see what color she was wearing underneath, but it was definitely her.

She looked just as surprised as he was. "What in the world are you doing here?"

CHAPTER 22

Ricky was convinced. It was like a nightmare come true.

"You're Carly?" He could barely squeak the question out. How could a terrible mix-up like this have happened?

She stared at him angrily. "What are you talking about?"

"Carly," he repeated. "With the tan sweater. I mean teal one."

She crossed her arms. "Have you been drinking?"

"No, it's just that … So you're saying you're not Carly?"

"Do I look like a Carly to you?"

"Maybe not, but I was going to meet someone here, and …"

"Ricky?" He turned around at the sound of his name.

"Sorry," he started to explain. "I'm waiting for

someone and ..." He stopped and squinted at her. Yup, that was definitely a turtleneck sweater.

But was it teal?

"Are you Ricky?" she asked again. He could hear the nervousness in her voice.

"Yeah. So you're Carly? I think there's been a mistake."

She laughed a little nervously. "No, I'm Carly. And if you're Ricky, then I think we're both at the right place. Soulmates, right?"

Ricky glanced back to where Jillian had been, but she was gone. Just as well. He was flustered enough already.

"Listen," he began, "there's something I should tell you."

"Okay. But should we get our seats first maybe?"

"Maybe. I mean, probably not. It's just that ..." He glanced around one more time, trying to figure out where Jillian had gone. He hadn't been trying to be rude.

He took in a deep breath. He could do this. "All right, there's something I need to tell you. Before we get a table."

She frowned. "Are you okay?" Fingering her hair, she asked, "Were you expecting me to look different or something?"

"No. You're fine how you look," he assured her

absently. He had to jump into what he really meant to say. "I just don't think you really want to date me."

"Holy cow. Are you gay?"

"Wait, what? No, I mean, I didn't ... No. Just listen." He clenched his sweaty palms. "It wasn't me you were emailing. It was my mother."

"What?"

He nodded. Now that his tongue was loose, he couldn't have tightened it to save his life. "She's kind of ... well, it's like this, see. She thought I should find someone to date. The girl I took to homeschool prom, she just got married, you know, and I guess Mom always thought that the two of us would end up together, but obviously we didn't, so she ... I'm botching this all up, aren't I?"

Carly bit her lip and adjusted the strap of her purse. "So you drove all the way out to Wenatchee to tell me I was really emailing your mom?"

"Yeah. I'm so sorry. I tried to send you a message through the Soulmate website, but your inbox was full ..." He let out his breath, finally able to look her in the eyes. "I'm so sorry. I didn't know she was doing it, honest. As soon as I found out, I tried to let you know. And if you still want to, you know, eat or something, I hear the breadsticks are really good here. But it's ... I just wanted to get that out in the open. And apologize again for wasting your time."

She stared at him. "Wow."

"Yeah," he agreed dejectedly. How did you go about ordering a table for one around here?

"No, I mean, wow," she repeated. "Nobody's ever been that honest on a first date before."

"Like I said, I'm really sorry I wasted your time. Hey, maybe if you want, I'll buy us some breadsticks to go and you can take some home with you so you don't get too hungry."

She frowned. "You mean you don't want to have dinner with me?"

"No, I mean, yeah, I'm starving, but I figured you wouldn't want to go on a date with someone you thought was a dude but turned out to be a middle-aged woman emailing you on her son's behalf and making you think that …"

"All right, enough about your mother already."

"Come again?"

"I said enough about your mother. I get it. Parents can be interfering pains in the neck. But that was really brave of you to come clean right away, and like I said, I've never had anyone be that open on a first date before. I've got to admit, I think it's kind of hot."

"You do? I mean …" Ricky stared at her turtleneck sweater, wondering why the Olive Garden turned on its heater in the middle of the spring.

"So should we stay for a while?" She wrapped her arm in his.

He gulped. "Yeah, I mean, sure. Why not, right?"

He started to charge ahead but she pulled him back.

"What is it?" he asked. "Did you change your mind already?"

She nodded toward the podium. "They haven't called our names yet."

"Oh." All the nervous energy he'd been storing up escaped in a laugh that was far too boisterous, but he couldn't help it. "Yeah, okay. Well, let's wait over here. This bench is pretty comfortable. I know that from personal experience."

CHAPTER 23

Ricky thought that once he and Carly were seated at their own table, he'd feel slightly less nervous.

He was wrong.

Fortunately, when he spilled his glass of ice water, both he and his new date managed to stay dry. That was a step in the right direction at least.

And when he banged his knee against the table, Carly reached over and rubbed it, asking gently if he'd gotten hurt.

Another positive sign.

He even managed to get through the part where you order your food off the menu without getting too tongue-tied. Maybe he was more cut out for this dating stuff than he'd given himself credit for.

Carly scooted a little closer to him on the bench they shared. "So tell me," she said, "how many of these dates has your mom set you up on?"

"Oh, this is my first," he answered before he thought to check her face to see if she was mocking him. With the lighting so dim and her leaning so close, it was hard to tell. He cleared his throat and scooted back an inch. "What about you? I mean, not about your mom setting you up, but dates like this. Have you been on Soulmates very long?"

She shrugged. "I've done all right."

"Do you get a lot of messages? I mean, that was my first thought when it kept telling me your inbox was full."

Another shrug. "I get enough, I guess. But right now, I'm not interested in any of that. I'm more interested in you."

She was so close he could smell something like strawberries on her breath. He cleared his throat again and reached for his water.

"Tell you what." Her hand was on his knee again, and she pressed up against him until he could feel each curve of her body.

Every one.

He reached for another drink of water, just barely managing to keep from spilling it down the front of that teal sweater she wore. As a turtleneck, it certainly covered everything up nicely, but as a sweater, and a fairly tight one at that ... Why were they blasting the heat in here?

He gulped down another sip of water. "So listen." He tried to move his shoulder over just a little, but there was no room between them now. "I, um, I think maybe we should sit across from one another, and then ..."

"I'm sorry," she crooned. "Am I making you *uncomfortable*?" She whispered the word in his ear, invoking a shiver reflex that started at the base of his spine and traveled all the way up to his neck.

"Listen," he tried again, but his words were interrupted by a curse from the table behind them. It was a rude enough remark to snap Ricky out of his near panic at sitting next to a woman who apparently wanted to climb onto his lap.

"Did you hear what that guy just said?" he asked.

Carly glanced back. "What, that? Just ignore them. Probably just a first date gone bad. Not at all like what we've got going on here, right? You'll have to thank your mommy for hooking us up."

"H-h-hooking up?" he stammered.

"Yeah. Or did you skip that class in homeschool?"

"No, it's just that I ..." His leg was going at about a hundred bounces per millisecond. There was something he had to sort out right away. "It's just that, I may as well tell you, I haven't dated all that much, so I guess I'm still a little new at this …"

"I like that about you," she said in a voice he could have sworn was lower than what it had just been.

"But see, I think I was picking up on the wrong signals. I'm a guy, you know."

"I did notice."

"And as a guy, my brain's a little bit … I don't know how I'm supposed to say this …"

"I can see that."

"Okay." He took one more sip of water even though his hand was shaking nearly as fast as his leg was bouncing. "Okay," he repeated. "This is going to sound really silly to you, but you said earlier you like honesty, right?"

"I dig it," she purred.

He laughed nervously. "Okay, well don't be offended or anything. I'm just laying it all out here, but I actually thought for a minute that … and this is going to sound totally crazy … but I seriously thought you were trying to come on to me."

The laugh he expected never came.

"Excuse me?"

"No, I mean, I know you're not really that type of girl, but before things get even more awkward …"

"Oh, we're way past awkward now, buddy."

Ricky wasn't all that good at reading a woman's body language or picking up on subtle changes in vocal inflection, but he was pretty sure that the way she said *buddy* meant that he'd done something wrong.

Unforgivably wrong.

"I'm sorry for offending you," he began. "Like I said, I know you're not really that sort of girl ..."

Carly was now so far to the other edge of the bench Ricky was ready to reach out and catch her if she lost her balance and fell off. She glared at him, and even in the restaurant's dim lighting, he could sense the anger in her expression. "Wait a minute, did your mom set up your profile for you?"

"Yeah. I already told you that. Is that why you're so upset and angry?" He was so confused. Hadn't they already moved past that first awkward confession?

"So your mom set up your profile page, and you have no idea what she put?"

"No. She did it all without me knowing. I already told you that."

Carly scoffed and grabbed her purse. "Great. Just great."

"What is it? What did I do?"

"It isn't what you did," she snapped. "It's what you

didn't do. Did you at least look at what she said about you?"

"Yeah. Once I found out about it at least. I was really curious about what she wrote." What had he done to upset her? Things seemed to have been going so well. Too well, in fact, but now, with Carly standing up and holding her purse, Ricky wondered if the date was about to end before he even got to try one of Olive Garden's famous breadsticks.

"So you read every single question she answered about you?" Carly pressed. "Even the heat scale?"

"Yeah. I'm a big fan of Mexican food. That's why I thought it was funny you suggested Olive Garden when your profile said you like hot and spicy too."

Carly whipped her hair out of her face. "Unbelievable," she huffed. "You and your mom both. You're totally unbelievable."

He stood up too when she took her first step to leave. "Wait a minute. Let's talk this through. I thought we had a good connection just a few minutes ago. I thought you liked me."

Carly pulled her keys out of her purse. "Listen, kid. A quick word of advice for both you and your mama. The next time you fill out one of those questionnaires, you forget all about hot and spicy and put down warm milk. Got that?"

"What are you talking about? I don't even drink milk. Why did you …"

"Have a good night." She tossed a five-dollar bill onto the table. "This covers my half of the tip."

It wasn't until then that Ricky realized how many other people at the restaurant were staring at him. He sat back down, wondering what was supposed to happen next and trying to decide if tasting an Olive Garden breadstick was worth the past ten minutes of humiliation.

CHAPTER 24

"Here you go, hon."

Ricky thanked the middle-aged waitress.

"Can I get you anything else?" she asked.

"Maybe one more basket of breadsticks?" he asked hopefully.

"No problem. And I talked to the manager. He said that since the young woman was gone by the time the food came out, we'll just charge you for one dinner instead of two."

Ricky grinned as best as he could with his mouth full of buttery garlic breadstick. As uncertain as he'd been a little earlier, he'd definitely made the right decision about staying for dinner after Carly stormed out.

The waitress left, and Ricky noted with a sense of pride that he hadn't spilled any of his soup or salad on the tablecloth or on himself.

"Yeah, well, when I take some gal out for a nice meal, it's only reasonable to expect a little something in return."

The man behind him had been talking at that obnoxiously loud volume ever since Ricky got his food. He couldn't hear the replies of the woman as clearly, but he'd picked up on enough to know that as poorly as his first date had gone with Carly, the woman behind him was in even worse shape.

"If you were just looking for a free meal, that's what welfare is for, babe. You think I make a ton of money? You think I'm in the habit of driving hours out of my way to pick up chicks and pay for a big expensive meal like this and then going home without so much as a thank you? Why would I have driven all that distance to pick you up if I wasn't expecting to take you home with me? That's not how I work, babe."

"Well, it's how I work," his date retorted. Ricky was glad she was finally standing up for herself. Someone needed to tell that jerk off.

"You think something like cramps is an excuse? You know how much this dinner cost?"

"Do you know how much I don't care?" she shot back.

Wait a minute. He recognized that voice.

"You know, the more we talk, the more I get the

impression that you went into tonight thinking you'd get a free meal without having to give anything in return."

"Congratulations, bozo," she said. "That was exactly my intention."

"Just what kind of brat do you think you are?"

Ricky turned around in his seat. There was no way he could sit by and let someone talk to any woman like that, especially not someone he knew.

"Hey," he said, forcing as much assertiveness into his tone as possible. "Hey, stop talking to her like that. When you're out on a date with somebody, you've got to treat her like a lady."

The man turned around and glared at him. "Who told you that? Your mama?"

"Actually," Ricky replied, "she … Never mind about that. Why are you bugging her so much?"

"What business is it of yours anyway? From what I saw earlier, you think I'm going to be taking dating advice from you?"

Ricky swallowed down his humiliation. "All I'm saying is you need to treat a lady with respect."

The man turned back around and slung his arm around Jillian. "I'll treat her right when she learns her place."

Jillian stood up on the bench. "That's it," she declared.

The man stared at her with wide eyes. "What do you think you're doing?" he asked. "Get down from there."

"No. I've asked you several times to scoot over and let me out, but since you're obviously a buffoon whose vocabulary is too limited to understand what I'm saying, I can just take care of it myself."

She stepped over the back of the seats until she was standing on the bench next to Ricky. "Mind if I join you?"

Ricky stared at her as she sat down beside him.

"What do you think you're doing?" the man behind them growled.

"Take a hint, buddy," Jillian flung back at him. "Our date just officially ended."

CHAPTER 25

"I'm really sorry," Ricky said.

Jillian reached out for another breadstick. "You don't have any reason to apologize. That guy's a jerk. The worst part of it is he's my ride all the way back home …"

"Not anymore."

Jillian looked like she was about to argue, then stared at the table. "Thanks."

"Don't mention it."

"It was really stupid of me. I didn't even tell my aunt where I was going. I just said I'd be out for a few hours. It could have ended really badly."

If Ricky hadn't known better, he might have thought there was a tremor in her voice.

"Well, the good news is you don't have to rely on him driving you home."

"Yeah, but now he knows where I live, and …"

Ricky waved his napkin, which landed partially in his water cup. "Don't worry about that. Jerks like him wouldn't waste the time it'd take to track you down."

"Thanks, I think." Jillian smiled.

Ricky wasn't exactly sure what was so funny, but he returned her grin. "You're welcome, I think."

"So I take it your date didn't turn out that hot either?" She let out a little chuckle. "Or maybe it was too hot, and that was the problem."

It felt good to be able to laugh about Carly. "I had no idea what was happening."

"Yeah, that's why they put those heat scale questions in there. Are you telling me your mom actually thought it had to do with what food you liked to eat?"

Ricky would rather die than confess he'd thought the same thing until the minute Carly stormed out of the restaurant.

He chuckled with Jillian, noting how much more relaxed he felt now that he was here with someone he already knew.

"I'm glad you showed up," he admitted. "I felt kind of strange eating my breadsticks all alone."

"You know they're going to charge us both now that there's two of us sharing the meal, right?"

Ricky shrugged. His dad had slipped him the credit card earlier, so he wasn't too worried. "I'll take care of it."

Jillian reached into her purse. "Let me cover my half, all right? After everything, it's the least I can do."

Ricky reached his hand out to stop her from digging into her purse. "No, really. Let me pay. I want to."

Jillian narrowed her eyes. "I said I'd take care of it." Her voice was a near growl.

"Oh." Ricky stared at her, wondering what had brought on the sudden transformation. Hadn't they been laughing just a few seconds ago?

She let out her breath, and stuck some money on the side of the table next to the five-dollar bill Carly had plunked down. Ricky was confused. Wasn't the man supposed to always pay for the meal?

He opened his mouth once more to protest, saw Jillian's set expression, and changed his mind. If his mom asked about the bill, he'd just say they got a special discount.

In a way, it was the truth.

Sort of.

"Hey, babe."

Ricky looked up to see Jillian's former date glaring down at them. "Good luck getting home. You know there's no way I'm making that drive twice."

She smiled. "Good night to you, too. I had a swinging good time," she added sarcastically.

He gave her a sickeningly sweet smile, turned to scowl at Ricky, and left.

"Where'd you find a winner like that?" Ricky asked.

"Just some website." She wiped her mouth with her napkin. "But let's forget about him. Tell me about your mom. Did she seriously set you up with your own dating profile?"

CHAPTER 26

After all-you-can eat breadsticks, soup, and salad, Jillian could swear she'd die if she tried to swallow down one more bite. So why was Ricky still trying to talk her into dessert?

"No, seriously," she insisted. "I really can't."

"Watching your weight?" he joked, and then his face fell. "I'm so sorry. I shouldn't have said that. I didn't mean …"

She studied his features, trying to guess how much he already knew.

"What exactly didn't you mean?"

"That you were the kind of girl who would have to watch her weight in the first place."

She let out her breath. Good. She was surprised that she'd made it through half a week in Orchard Grove without the pregnancy becoming common knowledge.

When she showed up in church on Sunday, she expected to end up as the primary subject of that week's prayer chain update.

Did you hear the McAllister girl's pregnant?

Who's the dad, I wonder.

I always said there was something off about that family.

What do you expect after what her father did?

She hated her dad for what he'd done to their family, and she hated her mom for sticking with him. Her father claimed his affair had been a one-time mistake and that was all, but Jillian didn't even care. After what he'd done — dragging their whole family through so much shame, making them move to a new town, costing them all their friends — she figured he didn't deserve to be forgiven. Maybe not the godliest of attitudes, but once she saw the way the people at Orchard Grove had crucified her entire family for her father's sin, she didn't care all that much anymore about what other Christians thought about her and her life choices.

At least she didn't have to deal with her parents now. Her father was the worst. As soon as she told him about the pregnancy, he'd done nothing but shake his head and pace the hallways, muttering under his breath, "Where did I go wrong?"

If he'd bothered to ask Jillian, she could have told him in less than five seconds.

"What about ice cream?" Ricky asked, interrupting her thoughts. "Do you think you have room for ice cream? Or frozen yogurt? We could find a frozen yogurt lounge."

"As fun as it's been," she said, wondering if the sarcasm would be lost on him, "I think I'm ready to head home. If that's okay with you."

He shrugged. "Sure. I honestly didn't expect my date to last even as long as it did, so if you're sure you don't want anything else to eat ..."

Just the thought of one more bite made her queasy. "I'm sure."

"Well, then, let's go." He led the way to his car.

"This is your ride?" she asked. "Sweet."

"It's my dad's, but he lets me use it."

He opened the passenger door for her then stood waiting for her to sit so he could hand her the seatbelt. On the surface, it seemed like a nice gesture, but it made her feel rushed, like the longer she took to get buckled, the more of his time she was wasting.

Oh, well. If he wanted to stand there by the curb looking like an idiot, who was she to try to stop him?

"What's your dad do?" she asked when he got into the

seat next to her.

"Oh, he has his own courier business." He turned to stare at her. "Didn't I already tell you that?

She shrugged. Next thing you know, he'd expect her to remember the name of the doctor who delivered him as a baby too.

"So you're okay?" he asked as they pulled onto the road. "You're not too upset about that jerk?"

"I'm fine. I've met plenty like him before. You get sort of used to it."

"I'm sorry."

She glanced at him, surprised by how genuine he sounded. "Yeah, well, don't worry about that. Speaking of bad dates though, that girl was literally all over you, wasn't she?"

He laughed sheepishly. If she weren't so tired, she'd tease him just to see how deeply she could get him to blush.

"It was a little awkward," he admitted.

"But you learned a lesson, right?"

He nodded. "Yeah. Don't let your mom fill out your dating profile. And make sure she knows what hot and spicy really means."

CHAPTER 27

"Aunt Connie, I'm home," Jillian called out as she kicked off her shoes. She had to get to the bathroom and find some supplies.

Uncle Dennis looked up from his newspaper with a frown. "Your aunt's worried."

"I told her I'd be gone a while."

"She's been waiting up for hours."

Jillian ignored her uncle's glare and peeked into the kitchen. "Connie?"

"She's out with the goats. Had to tuck the kids in all by herself tonight."

Jillian pulled her fashion boots back on. Not exactly the best for barn chores, but she didn't want to run all the way to the back porch to find the right pair, not with her stomach this upset. Why had she eaten so many breadsticks?

When she got to the barn, the door was already shut, but she couldn't see her aunt anywhere. Funny. Had she stopped by the gift shop to make sure everything was locked up tight?

"And you're going to sleep well like a good little baby, aren't you, sweet thing?"

Jillian strained her ears. Was that sound coming from inside the barn?

She rapped gently on the door. "Aunt Connie?"

The wooden panel slip open, and her aunt slipped out. "So there you are." She wrapped Jillian in a hug that smelled far too goaty for her comfort. "Your uncle and I were worrying our heads off over you."

"Sorry. I thought I said I'd be out for a little bit."

"An hour or two, that's what I think of as a little bit. It's past sundown," Connie exclaimed, as if the entire population of Orchard Grove was made up of enchanted mortals who would turn into vampires if they stayed out after dark.

"I'm sorry for worrying you." After the long night she'd already had, it was hard to make her voice sound sincere. She gave her aunt one more hug, hoping it might earn her a little bit of leniency. "Next time I'll be sure to call and check in, all right?"

"Well, you better head to bed now, but tomorrow we're going to need to have a long talk about your curfew. It's not appropriate for a young woman in your condition to be out so late. Who were you with anyway?"

At least this time she had an answer she thought her aunt would approve of. "Ricky Fields from church."

"You were out with Ricky Fields?" Connie stared at her with wide eyes. "Does his mother know?"

Jillian had to stifle down a laugh. Somehow she had the feeling Ricky might not tell his mom every sordid detail about his night out on the town.

CHAPTER 28

Jillian woke up with cramps and stared at the clock. Who was making so much noise at two in the morning? Was that one of the goats? It sounded like it was coming from outside.

She had to go to the bathroom anyway. Why hadn't that pregnancy center nurse warned her about all this second-trimester spotting? Well, there'd be no way she could go back to sleep until the racket died down, so she got out of bed, pulled on some yoga pants and a sweatshirt, and headed to the downstairs bathroom. For a minute, she thought that maybe Grandma Lucy was in her rocking chair, so she made a quick detour to check, but the prayer room was empty and dark. She slipped on her shoes and used her cell phone as a flashlight as she made her way to the barn.

When she got outside, she confirmed the noise was

coming from the goat pen, but she'd never heard an animal sound like that. She hesitated for just a moment before sliding the barn door open.

It wasn't the animals. It was her grandmother, on her knees in the hay, hands stretched up toward the rafters. Moonlight shined in from outside and lit up the tears on her cheeks. She was so caught up in her prayer that she didn't even notice Jillian peering in.

"Father God, lover of my soul, healer of all my sickness and sorrows, you know how much my granddaughter needs you, Lord. You know how lost and hurting she is, the way that she blames you for the way your people turned their backs on her and her family so many years ago. I confess the bitterness left in my own heart for the way my daughter and grandchildren were treated at a time when they were in so much need of your love and grace. Forgive me for all my faults, for all the ways I failed to pray for my grandchildren like I should. And now I see how my granddaughter resents you, how lost and hurting and broken she is, and I don't know what to say to her. I don't know how to reach her. It is only your Holy Spirit who can open her blind eyes so that she can see the depth of the love you have for her. It is only your truth that can show her that you are gracious and forgiving. She's gotten such a poor taste of how your children should love each other, and I confess that sometimes I fear the pain she's experienced at the hands of other believers is enough to threaten her faith for good. And so I'm asking you to hear my prayer and heal my granddaughter from all the wounds that have been inflicted on her in the name of righteousness and godliness. Show her that you are love and that you have no part in the judgmental, hypocritical attitudes that she's been exposed to her entire life. I don't want to see her hurting anymore, Lord."

She opened her eyes and stared straight at Jillian without a hint of surprise. How long had Grandma Lucy known she was standing there?

"Come here, child."

Jillian obeyed. What else could she do?

"I heard a sound," Jillian tried to explain. "I thought one of the goats might be in trouble."

"That's why I come out here," Grandma Lucy replied with a smile. "I've been known to be a little noisy in my prayers, and I'm sure that Connie and Dennis would rather get a full night's sleep than listen to this old lady's tears."

"What were you crying about?" It was a stupid question, but Jillian wanted to pretend that she had just entered and hadn't heard a word of her grandmother's prayer.

Grandma Lucy smiled. "I was just doing what I do every night when I can't sleep. Praying about the ones I love."

ALANA TERRY

CHAPTER 29

"I think Peaches has really taken a liking to you," Grandma Lucy remarked.

Jillian had lost track of how long she and her grandmother had spent in the barn. It might have been five minutes or thirty, but she couldn't even remember all that they talked about. Grandma Lucy would make a comment about one of the goats or ask Jillian something about her family, and then all of a sudden she'd break out into prayer, and then when she was finished, she'd go right back to her conversation with Jillian without so much as an *amen*. It was sometimes hard to figure out if she was talking to God or someone else at any specific moment.

"What does Connie have planned for you to do tomorrow?" she asked. "Are you working in the store all day?"

Jillian shook her head. "I have that doctor appointment

129

first thing in the morning."

Grandma Lucy nodded her head. "How are you feeling? How is your health?"

Jillian could think up a dozen other things she'd rather talk about than the pregnancy, especially now when she felt so crampy. Just another reminder of how someone else had taken over her body. "It's gotten a little easier now that I'm not so nauseous." That part was the truth, but the bleeding she'd been experiencing on and off for the past couple days was nearly as annoying as her periods had been.

Grandma Lucy shook her head. "I mean in here." She reached out and touched Jillian's chest.

She shrugged. "I just want to get it over with and move on."

"Pregnancy is a beautiful thing," Grandma Lucy breathed. "So many lessons you can learn through it all — love and grace and endurance."

Jillian shrugged again. "Maybe, but since I'm not keeping the baby, I don't really see it like that. It just feels like something that I have to get through, then life can go on like normal."

"So normal is good?" Grandma Lucy asked the question so pointedly that Jillian found herself responding defensively.

"It's better than here at least." She felt her shoulders sag, and she let out her breath. "I didn't mean that quite the way it sounded. I mean, I'm really thankful to you and Connie and Uncle Dennis for a place to stay and stuff, it's just that ..."

"It's just that Seattle is your home, and you miss your life, and you miss your classes at school, and you miss your friends," Grandma Lucy finished for her.

"Yeah. That pretty much sums it up."

"I know." Grandma Lucy said the words with such finality that Jillian didn't even bother questioning how she could be so certain. As long as she could remember, her grandmother had been exactly like this. Spiritual, intuitive. That's why it was so bizarre hearing her talk about her life before she got serious about her relationship with Christ.

"You know what I think?" Grandma Lucy asked and then continued on without waiting for an answer. "I think that if I were in your situation, I would feel more comfortable at my own home, surrounded by my own family and friends, not back in a town that held so many painful memories from my past."

Jillian picked up a piece of straw and rolled it between her fingers.

"You know what else I think?" Grandma Lucy

continued, and Jillian didn't bother to answer. "I think that what this town did to your mother and to you and your brother — and yes, even your father — was a real shame, and I pray every single day the God will one day heal those hurts and bring peace and comfort to your soul once again."

CHAPTER 30

"Jillian? Dr. Morrison's ready to see you now."

Jillian grabbed her purse, and her aunt stood up as well. "Do you want me.to go back with you?"

She shook her head. "I'll be fine." What did Connie think, that being pregnant made her forget how to follow a nurse and walk down a hall?

The Orchard Grove Family Medical Center was just as drab as she remembered it, even more so since she wasn't in the colorful pediatrics area anymore.

"Right down this way, if you please."

Jillian didn't know how many cups of coffee the nurse had consumed before her shift, but she swore there was no human explanation for why anybody should be this chipper so early in the morning.

Jillian had finally gotten herself back to bed after her long talk and prayer time in the barn with Grandma Lucy, but her body felt every single one of those lost minutes of sleep. What had she been thinking? Couldn't she have let her grandmother spend the night in the barn without having to go in and check on her?

And in the end, their conversation had only left Jillian feeling even guiltier that she wasn't the kind of Christian Grandma Lucy wanted her to be.

"Have a seat," the nurse told her, "and Dr. Morrison will be with you in just a few minutes."

Jillian stared at the white walls and wondered how long this appointment would take. At the Seattle pregnancy center, she talked to the nurse for nearly an hour. Most of that was about how her family would react to the news. She didn't bother to mention the real story of how she'd ended up in this situation.

What would it change?

Absolutely nothing.

She strummed her hands on the crinkly paper spread across the exam table. All Jillian wanted to know was that she was healthy and fine, and then she'd get going. She was working at the gift shop for Connie this afternoon, and it was time for her to finally read through those adoption pamphlets. She'd have to start making some choices soon.

Dr. Morrison came in, clipboard in hand, his face in a

drawn-out frown. "You're Jillian McAllister?"

She nodded.

"And you're in your second trimester?"

Why had she spent all that time filling out his paperwork if he was just going to make her repeat everything again?

"How do you feel?" he asked. "Any changes?"

She shrugged. "Some cramps. And spotting. It was heavier today than it was before." She was stupid to have avoided pregnancy research for so long. Maybe he could give her some pamphlets or magazines. She didn't need any more surprises over the next six months.

He frowned and pulled out his swivel chair. "Yeah, on that note, I want to talk to you about the results from your urine test."

CHAPTER 31

As hard as he tried, Ricky couldn't get her out of his head. Out of all the restaurants in Wenatchee, what would be the chances that they'd both meet their blind dates at the same place at the same time? And even more providential was the way he was able to drive her home so she didn't have to spend a second longer with that jerk she'd met online.

God must have had his hand in it all. Ricky was certain.

His mother had been waiting up for him when he got home — no surprises there — but Ricky had feigned a bad headache and went straight upstairs. He knew in the morning she would demand the details about his date, which is exactly what happened. Ricky answered as honestly as possible without mentioning the fact that he'd traded out partners halfway through the night and ended up having a great time with none other than Jillian McAllister, the wayward pastor's daughter.

Mom would never understand. As she saw it, Jillian was part of that taboo family whose father had done that Awful Thing so many years ago. There was no grace or forgiveness or second chances for people like them, even though it had been Pastor Joel who sinned and not his family.

So Ricky kept the secret about last night to himself, closed his Soulmates account, and wondered when he should ask Jillian out on a second date, this time where they'd hopefully both start as well as end the night together.

The more they had talked in the car last night on the long drive home from Wenatchee, the more Ricky realized that he'd been right about Jillian. She was lonely, but he still couldn't figure out what she was doing back in Orchard Grove. Grandma Lucy had fallen ill a few months ago but seemed to be in as good health as ever now, and it wasn't his place to question. Maybe she just needed a break from city life.

He was half an hour into his shift at work when his dad called his cell. "You made that delivery to Murphy's yet?"

"Almost. I'm on my way now. Just turned off Main Street."

"Good. After that, I want you to go home and pick up your mother. She has an appointment with the doctor."

"Is she okay? She didn't say anything to me about any appointment."

"She dropped a plate on her toe unloading the dishwasher this morning," his father answered. "She thinks it might be broken."

"Yes, sir." Ricky pulled into his next stop. "I'll run this in and pick her up right away."

"Good," his dad answered. "Don't be late now. You know how she feels about being on time."

CHAPTER 32

"I'm getting too old for this," Mom complained as she hobbled on her crutches to the elevator door. "I can hardly stand these things."

"I'm sorry." Ricky wondered if there was anything he could do to help. "Want me to run upstairs and see if they have a wheelchair you can borrow?"

"Mercy, no. The last thing I need is for the whole town to see me getting pushed around in one of those contraptions like an invalid. Now hold that elevator open. You know I'm terrified of those doors closing in on me."

Ricky did as he was told. "Which floor are you going to?" he asked.

"Two." Mom said the word sharply, as if she were disappointed her son couldn't keep track of every single medical provider she went to see in any given month. Especially from her battle with breast cancer, it seemed like the past decade had been one string of doctor visits after another.

No wonder she told him to work hard and always get good health insurance.

"Hold the elevator," a man called out, and Ricky pushed the button to keep the doors from closing.

He recognized that face.

"Good morning, Ricky." Susannah Peters (actually, she was Susannah Phillips now, even though he could never get that straight in his head) stepped into the elevator. She was holding the arm of her new husband, Scott, who gave Ricky and his mother friendly nods of greeting.

"How are you today?" he asked.

"Think I broke my foot," Mom muttered.

Susannah made a sympathetic face and was about to say something, but her new husband spoke instead. "We're here to get an ultrasound."

Ricky blinked. He remembered his mom getting a few of those tests over the years. Did that mean Susannah had breast cancer? She was so young, and she'd just married. "Is everything okay?" he gasped.

Susannah let out a cheerful, musical laugh. "We're having a baby." She beamed lovingly up at Scott.

"The two of you certainly didn't waste any time," Mom

muttered. "When's the due date?"

Susannah answered, and Ricky watched Mom stare at the elevator ceiling while making mental calculations. "Oh," she eventually exclaimed, apparently satisfied. "Well, congratulations to you both."

"Yeah," Ricky repeated after her. "Congratulations."

And he felt the heat rushing to his ears but didn't know why. He was thankful when the elevator doors finally opened.

"Are you two getting off here?" Scott asked.

Ricky nodded and helped his mom hobble on her crutches off the elevator. At least Susannah and her new husband were going up one more floor. Ricky didn't know why he should be embarrassed at the news of a newly married couple expecting their first child, but he was glad that he wouldn't have to make any more chitchat with either of them.

The doctor's office was just across the hall from the elevator, and he held the door open while Mom maneuvered on her crutches to the waiting area. "You check me in," she told him. "I'm already exhausted just from that elevator ride."

By the time Ricky sat down, Mom was having a noisy conversation with Connie, Jillian's aunt. What was she doing here? And what if she mentioned his date with her niece?

"Oh," he stammered, "I have my next delivery right around the corner and ..." He cleared his throat. "I think I've got time to run there real quick and get back in just a few minutes." He handed his mom the clipboard, dropped the pen, and then knocked over two magazines from an end table when he tried to straighten himself up. Without waiting for permission to leave or offering any other explanation, he headed out the door as fast as he could manage without tripping over both legs.

CHAPTER 33

The ten minutes that Ricky said it would take to make his next delivery turned into half an hour, and he still lingered in the first floor lobby of the Orchard Grove Family Medical Center a few more minutes before he found the nerve to head back up to his mom. Whatever Jillian's aunt may or may not have said about last night, Ricky couldn't do anything to change that. It was his own fault for thinking he could keep secrets so big in a town this small.

Oh, well. His one night out with Jillian had been great. Too bad his mom would never dream of allowing him to take her out on a second date.

But wait a minute. Hadn't he been telling himself all week that he didn't have to live like that anymore? Hadn't his experience Sunday at church taught him there were more important things — far more important things — than fearing Mom's disapproval?

He didn't have to hide from her. And he didn't have to get her permission before asking Jillian out again. In fact, by the time the elevator doors opened and he was standing in front of the doctor's office, he decided that he was going to ask Jillian tonight if she wanted to go out with him over the weekend.

Mom might object — and probably would — but as long as Ricky wasn't doing something outside of God's word, what did it matter?

He wiped his hands on his pants, took a deep breath, and walked into the lobby. Mom wasn't there. Good. That meant she was still with the doctor and wouldn't be mad at him for returning late.

"Well, did you get your deliveries made?"

He turned toward the voice, bumping into the back of one of the chairs in the process.

"Oh, hi, Connie. Is my mom still with the doctor?"

She nodded and patted the seat next to her. "How are you doing today?"

"I had a really good date with Jillian last night," he blurted out before his brain could catch up with his tongue. "We ate a lot of breadsticks."

Connie looked a little bit surprised.

"She's a really tasty girl," he hurried to continue. "And the breadsticks were fun. I mean, no wait, it's the other way around."

Connie raised her eyebrows. "So the two of you really were out last night?"

Ricky wasn't sure what to make of the disbelief in her expression, but he nodded. "Yeah, did she tell you about that jerk she met at the restaurant?"

A minute or two later, he had given Connie nearly every detail he could recall leading up to Jillian's ditching her date at Olive Garden and joining Ricky at his table instead.

"She didn't tell me any of that," Connie finally admitted.

"Oops. Maybe she didn't want you to know. Might be best if you could pretend you didn't hear all of that from me. But would it be all right with you if I asked her out again?" His leg was bouncing, and he put a magazine on his lap in hopes that the little bit of extra weight would calm down his nerves.

"Well, that's fine with me, but you know you'll have to ask her yourself."

"What? Do you think she doesn't like me? Did she say something about it?"

"No, it's nothing like that." For the first time, Connie looked as flustered as he felt. "You'll just have to ask her yourself. That's all I can say."

Ricky felt his expression fall and remembered how embarrassed he'd been last night when Carly dumped him. He didn't want anything like that to happen again, especially not with Jillian. Was this Connie's way of telling him not to get his hopes up? Was she trying to soften the blow or drop some sort of hint? If only he could read women better.

Connie sighed. "For what it's worth, hon, I would be very happy to see you and Jillian spending more time together. But of course, you know it's not my choice to make. All that's up to my niece."

"What's up to me?" Jillian's apparent materialization out of nowhere made Ricky shoot to his feet, dropping the magazine for pregnant women that had been on his lap.

"What's up to me?" Jillian repeated.

Connie buried her head in her purse while she rummaged around. "Oh, it's nothing, dear. Ricky and I were just talking, that's all. "

"Talking about me? What did you say?" She shot Ricky a glare, which he wished he could better decipher. Why did it seem like any time he talked to Jillian he said something wrong or made her mad?

"Ricky was just telling me about the way that …"

"I wanted to ask you out again," he blurted, unable to keep the words down any more than he could have kept his leg from jostling a few minutes earlier. "How about ice cream sundaes at The Creamery on Saturday? I'm off work at two."

He held his breath, wondering if it would be always be this terrifying to talk to girls or if it miraculously managed to get easier over time.

Jillian shook her head. "Not Saturday."

"Why not, dear?" Connie inserted. "I've known this boy since he was in diapers, and I can assure you he's a fine young man and one any woman would be proud to call her beau."

Jillian glowered, and Ricky noticed for the first time that she was wearing one of those turtleneck sweater things like Carly had. Maybe it was some sort of trend.

"First of all," she explained, "I'm never going to call anybody my *beau* because I'm not over the age of a hundred. And second, I won't be free Saturday, so thanks anyway but no thanks."

"Jillian," her aunt snapped.

Ricky reached out, trying not to knock anything over in

the process. "Well, if Saturday doesn't work, how about Sunday? I can take you out for burgers after church."

"Not then either."

"Why not?" Connie demanded. Ricky couldn't tell if having her aunt speak improved his chances or just made them worse.

"I'm not going out with you on Saturday or Sunday or any other day of the week because I'm leaving this stupid town, and I swear I'm never coming back again."

CHAPTER 34

"What part of *I don't want to talk about it* is difficult for you to understand?" Jillian had never snapped like that at her aunt before, but during the entire car trip back to Safe Anchorage, Connie had done nothing but pry into her personal life, trying to butt her head into what was absolutely none of her business.

"All you need to know is I'll be back at Seattle by the end of the week. Sorry, but you'll have to find someone else to help you in the gift shop."

"I just wish you'd let me know what …"

"I said I don't want to talk about it." Jillian clenched her jaw shut, focusing on that instead of the tightness in her throat. Why couldn't people in this stupid town learn to mind their own business? Why couldn't they take no for an answer, and why did they have to keep on pushing and pushing and pushing?

When did no stop meaning no, and how could Jillian convince everyone around her, especially her aunt, that there was no way to force someone into talking about things they didn't want to talk about? Repeating yourself multiple times or sugaring the questions with that sickeningly sweet tone just made things worse.

"Well," Connie finally sighed, "I think at the very least you owe Ricky Fields an apology." She held her hand up and continued before Jillian could protest. "I'm not saying you have to go out with him. That's up to you, but I'd be willing to guess you're the very first girl he's ever gotten the nerve up to ask out on a proper date, and he did it without wetting his pants or knocking over every single chair in that doctor's office, and he at least deserves some decency and respect when he gets turned down. And I know it's none of my business, but like I already said, he's the kind of man any girl should be proud to call her beau."

"Will you please stop using that word?" Jillian snapped. "No matter how hard you people here in this backwards town don't want to admit it, we're all the way in the twenty-first century now. A girl doesn't have to go out with the guy just because he's got a good reputation or asks nicely. And she certainly doesn't have to put out just because someone buys her an expensive meal."

Connie gasped. "What on earth are you talking about now?"

Jillian crossed her arms. "Never mind. I just want to get home and get my bags packed and figure out how I'm going to get back to Seattle."

"Does this have anything to do with what the doctor told ..."

"I said it's none of your business." Jillian glowered out the window muttering, "When will you people learn to leave others alone?"

CHAPTER 35

It was nearly dinnertime before anyone dared venturing up the attic staircase to knock on Jillian's door. At least her relatives had shown the decency to give her some space. She would offer up some sort of apology at dinner, Connie would forgive her and wrap her up in a hug, and it would be just like the ending of some cheesy family sitcom from the 90s.

At least she had a way back to Seattle. Sunday morning, one her friends from college would be visiting his mom. He could stop by Orchard Grove on his way back to Seattle and take Jillian home.

About stinking time.

Another knock. At least back at her own house she had a lock on her door. Not that she planned to stay at her parents' for much longer. If the failed experiment of this past week in Orchard Grove had taught her anything, it was that she needed to be out on her own, or at least living with people her age. She'd already dropped out of spring semester thanks to her parent's ingenious plan of hiding her away like a nun in a convent, but she could spend the summer working and save up enough so that by fall she could afford one of the apartments off campus. Anything to get away from her prying family.

"Can I come in?"

Jillian was surprised to see Grandma Lucy. Until now, she hadn't even known her grandmother could still maneuver up the steep and narrow staircase.

"Sure."

Grandma Lucy crossed her arms and scowled. "And what do you think you're doing, locking yourself up here all day and throwing a pity party for yourself? Is that any way for a king's daughter to behave?"

So maybe this wouldn't turn into a hug fest like on a sappy sitcom after all.

"I know, Grandma. I wasn't really thinking …"

"I'm not finished," Grandma Lucy stated tersely. "Your Aunt Connie has spent this past week going dozens of extra miles for you. She's taught you how to milk and trained you to work in her store so you had some source of income, and she's taken you to the doctor to make sure you're healthy, and she stayed up hours later than normal last night worrying about you when you didn't even have the decency to say you were going to be out late. And maybe you think that just because Connie is a righteous, God-fearing woman that you can take advantage of her like that, but the last I checked, this house is still listed under my name, which means if you're staying here, you're doing things by my rules. Whether you like it or not, you're part of our family, and that means that when you're hurting or angry or upset about something, you talk with us about it so we can pray with you and encourage you. You don't sit up here and pout like a spoiled little baby. Do you understand me?"

Jillian blinked and nodded. She had never seen Grandma Lucy like this and wouldn't even have guessed that it was possible for her to be anything but a sweet, little, soft-spoken old lady with shock white hair and spectacles who sat around in her rocker all day praying to an invisible God.

"Well then, if you don't want to tell your aunt Connie what's troubling you, you're going to have to tell me."

"I'm really not ready, Grandma." Jillian wasn't trying to be sassy anymore. In fact, all her energy was spent on trying to keep her tears from betraying her.

"Then you better make yourself ready, little missy, because no granddaughter of mine gets to waltz in here and live rent free and hurt her aunt's feelings and then expect to come downstairs as if nothing at all happened. Bottom line is you tell me why you're acting like this, or you don't eat any dinner."

"You can't do that."

"Whose house did I just say this is? You may be an adult now, but you're living here as a guest under my roof, and no guest or granddaughter of mine is going to ..."

"Fine." Jillian interrupted before Grandma Lucy had the chance to jump into yet another lecture. Who would have thought a woman that age could have so much attitude packed into her little four-foot-ten frame?

Grandma Lucy knitted her eyebrows together. "So you're ready to finally talk?"

Jillian sighed heavily. No, she wasn't ready, but it wasn't as if her grandmother was giving her any other choice.

Grandma Lucy sat down on the side of the bed and crossed her legs beneath her. Another surprise. Jillian wondered if she would be that agile when she was so old.

Her grandmother stared at her pointedly. "Well, I'm listening."

CHAPTER 36

Whoever said that confession was good for the soul was either a lying idiot or had never been in a situation like Jillian's. After telling Grandma Lucy about her doctor's visit, she waited expectantly for something to happen. A hug — cheesy as it would be — a word of encouragement, even another lecture.

Instead, silence.

Grandma Lucy just sat there with her feet crossed and eyes closed. For a second Jillian was worried that she'd had a heart attack and died sitting up.

"Grandma?" she asked faintly.

"Father God," Grandma Lucy croaked.

Great. More prayers. Part of her wished that Grandma Lucy would stop wasting her time. If prayer alone really could help, didn't she think that it would have worked by now?

"You see how much my granddaughter is suffering, and you know the sorrow and the confusion that are raging war against her soul. You alone know the powers of darkness that are threatening to consume her in bitterness and anger and self-pity. I declare, Father God, in the holy and mighty name of Jesus Christ whose blood takes away the sins of the world, who defeated death, hell, and the grave, that Jillian is not a slave to fear. She is not a slave to bitterness. She is not a slave to anger. All the hurts, all the wrongs that have been done to her, you will avenge them, Lord. You are a just and mighty God, and you repay wickedness, and we rejoice that we have you on our side as a faithful and almighty warrior. We rejoice that one day you will destroy all wickedness with just one word from your mouth. Hallelujah.

"I don't pretend to know everything that my granddaughter has gone through or what she must be feeling right now, Lord, but that's just fine because you are the one who knit her together in her mother's womb. You are the one who is intimately familiar with all her ways. You are the one who sent your Son to redeem her from the curse of sin and to offer her true and abundant life through Jesus Christ, our precious and merciful Savior.

"You've seen her while she wanders, Lord, and just like

the good Shepherd that you are, you are calling her back into your fold once again. And now, God, I pray that all the hurt that she's experienced at the hands of your children would be healed by the power of the blood of Jesus Christ. I declare that anger and bitterness have no root in my granddaughter's heart, but all the pain she's been holding onto for so long is released and washed away in the name of Jesus Christ, and all the mistakes and sins of her past are thrown into the sea of forgetfulness and removed from her as far as the east is from the west, just as your good Word declares.

"I speak new life over my granddaughter today, joyful life, abundant life. May she be satisfied in you and in you only. May she know the deep and abiding love you have to offer her, and may she never doubt that all your plans for her are good."

Jillian blinked back her tears. Ever since she'd been a little girl, she had heard her grandmother pray like this, but tonight something stirred in her spirit like it never had before. If Grandma Lucy experienced even a fraction of this spiritual intensity, this heavenly power when she prayed, it was no wonder she spent so many hours a day crying out to God.

Jillian had never been all that overly affectionate, but

she reached out to take her grandmother's hand in hers, trying to find words that might convey how special that moment had been for her, how encouraged she was to know that she had someone in her life who would pray for her with that sort of intensity and fervor.

She gave her grandmother's hand a squeeze and whispered, "Thanks."

Grandma Lucy didn't answer.

"Grandma?" Her voice was quiet and trembling. She could hear the fear in it. "Grandma?" she asked again, louder this time.

Grandma Lucy's eyes fluttered open. She made a face that looked like she was gasping, but no breath came in.

"Are you all right?" Jillian asked. "Grandma Lucy?"

She jumped up from her bed, threw the door open, and hollered down the stairs. "Aunt Connie! Aunt Connie! Come quick. Hurry. Something's wrong with Grandma."

CHAPTER 37

"Did you hear about Grandma Lucy?" Ricky burst through the doorway and into the kitchen where Mom was fixing dinner.

"Of course I did. Who do you think has been updating the prayer chain? I've had so many phone calls I nearly burned the biscuits."

"Forget the biscuits. Isn't there something we can do?"

"Do? Did you all of a sudden get a medical degree without telling me? Do you know how to cure a woman's failing heart?"

"It's her heart?" Ricky asked. "I didn't know. I just heard that she was at the hospital again. Dad said there was an ambulance in front of Safe Anchorage, and he saw them carrying her out on a stretcher. What is it? Is it serious?"

His mother sighed. "The way I see it, that woman's past her time if you ask me." She shrugged and focused on chopping her onions. "Far as I can tell, if the doctors can't help her, there's nothing to be done."

"What about Jillian?" Ricky blurted without thinking.

Mom's expression turned icy. "What does that girl have to do with any of this?"

"It's her grandmother."

Mom pulled out a sharp knife and examined it. "Grandmothers die every day."

Ricky reached for the keys he had dropped onto the counter, dragging his sleeve through a bowl of salsa his mom had left out. "I better go see her."

"They're taking her straight to the ER. They're not going to let you just waltz in for a visit."

"Not Grandma Lucy," Ricky explained as he rammed into a dining room chair in his haste to get out the doorway. "Jillian. Be back later."

Mom called out after him, but he didn't slow down. He was probably Jillian's only friend right now in Orchard Grove. He wasn't going to let her go through a struggle like this alone.

"Hold it right there," Mom shouted again.

Ricky stopped with his hand on the doorknob.

Mom came around the corner, wiping her hands on her apron. "There's something you need to know before you go chasing after that McAllister girl."

Ricky sighed with annoyance. "She has a name, you know."

Mom shrugged. "Name or no name, that's still no excuse for someone in her situation to be pregnant."

CHAPTER 38

Pregnant? Was he hearing things? Was his brain playing tricks on him?

"What are you talking about?" He shoved his car keys into his pocket.

"I said that girl was pregnant. Didn't I warn you about getting involved with the likes of her?"

"How do you know?" Ricky asked. "Did someone tell you?"

"What else would a girl her age be doing at Dr. Morrison's office? He's the only one in town who delivers babies." She crossed her arms against her chest. "So tell me why should she be going to see him if it weren't about a pregnancy?"

Ricky shook his head. "No, there's got to be someone else, because Susannah went up today to the third floor, remember?"

Mom huffed. "Susannah's mother was one of those homeopathic nut jobs, and I'm sure Susannah and her husband were going up to see the midwife. Which doesn't change the fact that Dr. Morrison is the only OB-GYN in town, and it was his nurse who called the McAllister girl back. I'm telling you, son, that girl is pregnant, and she's trouble. So come in and eat your dinner and be a sensible child for once."

Jillian? Pregnant? He tested the thought, turned it around, mulled it over. Maybe it was true, but how did that change the fact that she was alone in a town full of people who hated her because of what her father had done? How did it change the fact that her grandmother was possibly dying of heart trouble or maybe already had, and Ricky was the only person in the entire town of Orchard Grove who might think to offer his support?

It didn't.

He pulled his keys back out of his pocket.

"Where do you think you're going?" Mom demanded.

"I already told you. I'm going to check on Jillian. Don't bother holding dinner for me either."

CHAPTER 39

Ricky wasn't sure what he had expected when he rushed out the door and sped to County Hospital. He probably pictured Jillian sitting there sobbing in the waiting room. She'd see him and throw her arms around him, and he'd hold her and let her cry until she started to feel better.

But when he got to the emergency room, all the nurse could tell him was that Grandma Lucy had been recently admitted, but only family members were allowed to visit.

"Is Jillian with her?" Ricky asked.

"I really couldn't say."

"Well, can I just go back and see?"

The nurse shook her head.

"Could you check for me?"

The nurse's phone rang, and she told Ricky to sit in a chair in the waiting room, which he did.

Twenty minutes later, he was still sitting.

What should he do? Had the nurse forgotten about him?

Should he remind her that he was waiting to see if Jillian was back there?

Then again, if Grandma Lucy was in such a serious condition, why would he expect Jillian to come out here when she hardly knew him instead of spending time by her grandmother's bedside where she belonged?

He certainly hadn't thought this through.

He glanced at the time. He'd wait twenty more minutes, and if he hadn't found her yet, he would just head home and face Mom.

Was it really possible that Jillian was pregnant? Wouldn't she have said something yesterday? Or maybe that wasn't the sort of thing you talked about on a first date.

Not like he would know.

And if she were pregnant, well … Ricky still had a lot to learn about the Christian life, but sleeping around was one of the major big deals.

"Ricky? Is that you?"

He jumped to his feet, and surprisingly nothing toppled over.

"Connie," he exclaimed. "I came by to hear how Grandma Lucy was doing. Is she okay?"

Connie shook her head. "It's another spell with her heart. The doctors have her on oxygen and monitors, and they say it could go either way."

He stared at his hands. What were you supposed to say to something like that?

"How's Jillian?" he finally asked. "I thought she might need someone to talk to."

"That's sweet of you to suggest, hon, but she's had a pretty hard day. I'm sure you understand."

"Oh." He shuffled from one foot to the other. "Okay, well, maybe you can just tell her I stopped by."

"I would love to tell her that, except I can't. She stayed back at the house, I'm afraid."

"She did? Maybe I should go check on her."

"I wish you would. I don't know what it is that got her upset earlier, but she and Grandma Lucy had been chatting for nearly an hour before everything happened, and it upset her so much that when we tried to talk her into coming to the hospital with us, she refused." Connie shook her head. "I wish I knew how to reach that girl."

"It's all right," Ricky told her. "I'll go and see how she's doing."

"I appreciate that, hon." Connie gave him a smile. Ricky was certain she was about to smother him amply, so he stepped back as quickly as he could, tripping over the heel of his shoe but managing to right himself before he landed in one of the chairs.

He cleared his throat. "I'll see you soon. I mean, maybe I'll see you soon." Why was he so breathless? He straightened himself out, made sure there was nothing else he was about to fall over, and panted, "I'm going to the house to check on her now. Bye."

CHAPTER 40

You're the stupidest girl in the state of Washington, Jillian thought to herself. Why had she told Connie she'd tuck these dumb goats in for the night?

She should be at the hospital with Grandma Lucy. Why had she refused to go?

The goats were just her excuse. She'd been afraid of what might happen, so she told Connie she'd stay home and take care of the animals. Well, everyone was in the barn now, those stupid goats with their loud bleating and smelly hay and stubborn ways. All except Peaches.

Jillian would kill that animal. She really would.

Jillian had been trying to coax her inside for half an hour at least. With one hand she held the barn door shut so all the other animals didn't escape, and with the other she kept stretching toward Peaches who stayed just out of reach.

Stupid animal.

Stupid farm.

Stupid town.

Well, at least she wouldn't have to stick around here anymore. Problem solved.

But what about Grandma Lucy? What if something happened to her ...

No, Jillian wasn't going to think like that. Grandma Lucy was a woman of prayer. God wouldn't let someone like her die.

Oh, who was she kidding? Women Grandma Lucy's age died all the time. In fact, it was something of a miracle Grandma Lucy hadn't passed away last winter when she'd had all those heart problems.

It wasn't fair. Jillian had told Grandma Lucy about the doctor's visit. Was that what finally killed her?

Was praying for Jillian Grandma Lucy's very last act on earth?

God, you can't take her away from me.

It was too terrible for Jillian to fathom. Who would pray for her once Grandma Lucy died? Who would spend hours in this barn, pouring her heart out to God for Jillian to heal from the wounds of her past?

Wounds not even Grandma Lucy knew about ...

I didn't tell her everything. Jillian shot out the prayer to heaven in a desperate attempt to catch the Lord's attention.

I didn't tell her everything! she repeated. *There's more I need to say.*

Jillian had suffered the past three months in lonesome, torturous silence. It's what her parents expected of her. It's what every lesson in her upbringing taught her.

You don't expose the dark and the hideous.

You smile and pretend like everything's all right.

Jillian went months refusing to talk about what happened. She hadn't even told her parents.

But she wanted Grandma Lucy to know.

Did you hear that God? You can't take her home yet.

Hot tears seared her cheeks. Peaches looked up at her with a mournful expression but still refused to step any closer.

God, don't let Grandma Lucy die.

She needs to know the truth.

CHAPTER 41

"Jillian? Are you out here?"

She tried to jump up. She didn't know who was here, but she didn't want them to find her sitting in a pile of dirty hay on a barn floor petting a stupid goat.

A goat who had finally allowed herself to be led into the barn once Jillian found some sunflower seeds to lure her in with.

"Jillian?"

Peaches was too heavy. Grateful for the coveted snack, the animal had nuzzled against Jillian until they both ended up on the ground, with Peaches resting her head comfortably on Jillian's lap.

There wasn't any time to move before the barn door opened.

She tried to hide her embarrassment. "Hey."

At least she was leaving Orchard Grove. She'd never

see Ricky again after tonight, so it shouldn't matter what he thought about stumbling in on her cuddling a goat. A goat who apparently thought it was a giant lapdog.

A giant, stinky lapdog.

"You okay?" He cocked his head to the side, and Jillian could just picture him wondering if she'd truly lost her mind.

Any longer stuck here in Orchard Grove, and she might.

"I'm fine. She's just ..." Jillian tried to push Peaches' head off her legs, but the goat refused to budge.

Stubborn animal.

Ricky squatted down beside her and scratched Peaches between the ears. Jillian could have sworn the goat wagged her tail.

"What are you doing here?"

Ricky cleared his throat. "I was just, you know. And your grandmother. At the County."

She stared at him. Was something wrong with her hearing, or had the poor boy lost the ability to communicate whatsoever?

He cleared his throat and tried again. "I went over to the hospital when I heard. About Grandma Lucy. I mean, your grandma, not mine. And, well, I got worried that maybe you were here lonely or maybe you wanted a ride to go see her or …" He let out his breath, and his shoulders sagged. "I thought maybe you could use a friend."

Jillian stared at the hay on the floor. Thoughtful as he was to come and check on her, he didn't need to see her turn into a hysterical mess.

Not now.

Not here.

Not him.

"That was nice," she replied. "But I don't need anything."

He continued rubbing the goat's head absently. "That's good. I mean, I was worried, and I wanted to check …" He didn't finish his thought, which was fine.

Jillian preferred the silence anyway.

"So." He lost his balance and ended up sitting on the floor beside her. Peaches snorted and rolled over slightly so her back was pressed up against him. "Do you want me to drive you to the hospital?"

Jillian let out her breath. The last place she wanted to be was there, with Grandma Lucy so sick and weak …

But hadn't she just prayed for the chance to tell her grandmother the full truth?

She stood up. Peaches' head plopped onto the floor.

The goat flicked her ears, then adjusted herself until she was resting on Ricky's lap.

Jillian dusted off her pants. She didn't want to look like a hillbilly covered in hay when she went to see her grandmother.

"Yeah," she said. "Let's go to the hospital."

CHAPTER 42

Ricky had a hard time understanding why he felt so protective of Jillian. If anything, shouldn't he be curious, trying to find out if she really was pregnant or not?

Then again, would it change anything? When she was ready to talk about it, she would. Right?

Not my business, he told himself as he opened the side door and helped her into his pickup.

If she moved out to Orchard Grove to avoid the gossip and everything else that would come from being a pregnant, unwed pastor's daughter, he didn't want to add to her problems.

Not my business, he repeated, reminding himself that their date really hadn't been a date after all, and the time he finally did get up the courage to ask her out for real, she'd turned him down.

Not my business.

It didn't matter if Jillian never saw him as anything more than the awkward, gangly boy who went to her father's church a long time ago.

What mattered was that she was all alone in a town of gossips who already had it out for her family. Her grandmother was being treated in the emergency room at County Hospital, and more than anyone else he could think of, Jillian McAllister needed a friend.

Everything else — her pregnancy (or at least the rumors of it), her rejection earlier today, her declaration that she was leaving Orchard Grove — was her business, not his.

He had one job right now. Get Jillian to see her grandmother. He'd do it for a stranger in a heartbeat, and he certainly wouldn't expect anything in return.

A friend.

He was being her friend.

The friend she so desperately needed.

And nothing more.

So why were his palms so sweaty he was worried his hands might slip off the steering wheel?

Not my business, he thought when he found himself wondering who the father of her child might be. And how long ago had she gotten pregnant, anyway? She certainly didn't look like she could fit a full-sized baby in there.

And what if his mom was wrong? There were lots of reasons a girl Jillian's age could end up at the doctor's office. He had to stop thinking about it. Clearing his throat, he searched his mind for something he could say. Anything to make conversation.

Talk about the weather. Ask her about her day …

"So has Grandma Lucy been pregnant for very long?"

Jillian snapped her head. "What?"

"I mean, *sick*. Her heart. I mean, has that been going on for very long?"

She crossed her arms. "That's not what you said."

His left leg was bouncing faster than a jackhammer. At least it wasn't the foot he needed for the gas.

He didn't dare look but felt her glaring at him.

He licked his lips. He had to explain himself. "I'm sorry. I was thinking about the goats and got Peaches mixed up with your grandmother."

This time, she didn't even bother to ask what he meant. Even though he kept his eyes fixed squarely on the road ahead, he felt her angry, accusing glower.

His skin prickled. This wasn't going well at all.

"That's not quite what I meant. I just remembered your aunt telling me you were pregnant … I mean, your aunt told me the goat was pregnant. Peaches, the goat, and then I was thinking about Peaches being pregnant — not you, because why would I think that? — but then I was wondering how your grandmother was, and sometimes my words get jumbled up with my thoughts, and it all gets a little confusing, and ..."

He wiped his sweaty palm on his jeans. "And, well, I'm sorry. I know your grandmother's not pregnant. But the goat is."

He let out a nervous chuckle then cleared his throat. "Sorry," he muttered.

When she didn't respond, he continued to flounder for the right thing to say. Anything to cover up such a terrible and embarrassing slip.

"So let me get this straight. Grandma Lucy's not pregnant, but the goat is. Did I finally get that right?"

Jillian's arms were crossed, her voice devoid of all emotion. "I guess it was stupid to think it could stay secret for long. You want to know the truth? Fine. I'll tell you."

WHAT DREAMS MAY LIE

CHAPTER 43

"Can we go now" Jillian asked with her hand on the door handle. "Please?"

She still hated herself for telling Ricky the truth. What business of his was it? But she was so worried about Grandma Lucy, so upset she hadn't told her everything. And Ricky had been treating her so kindly, even after she was rude earlier.

Then he looked so sad when she mentioned the urine test, how she'd started bleeding earlier that day, and then the entire story came pouring out.

Every detail.

Including how she ended up pregnant to start with.

Did he realize he was the only person in the world who knew?

But he promised not to tell anyone and seemed so earnest. Earnest and compassionate and concerned.

So why did she feel even worse now that the truth was out in the open?

Now that they were here in front of the hospital, all Jillian wanted to do was go see her Grandma and forget about how stupid she'd been to tell her entire life history to a near stranger.

Ricky hopped out of the truck. "Wait there," he said. "I'll come let you out."

Jillian rolled her eyes and opened the door for herself while he wrestled with the seatbelt that was holding his sleeve hostage.

"Are you okay?" he asked when he saw her standing on the curb. "Do you need anything?"

I need to go see my grandmother. She left the thought unspoken.

She headed toward the hospital entrance, and he sprinted to catch up to her. "Are you going to make it? I mean, is it painful or anything?"

She shrugged. "Doctor said it'll pass out on its own, probably in the next few days."

She didn't glance over to gauge his reaction. Whatever little schoolboy crush Ricky might have had on her, he certainly would realize by now that she wasn't his type.

Jillian knew exactly what became of boys like Ricky

Fields. They became nice, respectable businessmen, and they married sweet, godly, mild-mannered Christian women who kept house and baked bread and raised half a dozen babies or more.

Not girls like Jillian. Girls who could talk about something like a miscarriage — something that would be devastating to a model Christian housewife — in such clinical terms without feeling anything at all.

No, that wasn't right either.

The moment Dr. Morrison failed to detect the heartbeat, she had felt something.

Relief.

No appointments or endless piles of paperwork with the adoption agency.

No stretch marks or bloating or weight gain.

No more indigestion.

No more forced exile here in Orchard Grove.

Dr. Morrison wanted her to make an appointment to confirm the miscarriage with an ultrasound, but what was the point? The spotting turned to bleeding an hour after the appointment. Her child was gone. She hadn't told her parents yet. After the way they kicked her out, she wasn't even sure she was going to.

Ricky held open the door to the hospital. She hesitated

for just a moment. Was she ready for this?

Well, it didn't matter.

Ready or not, Jillian wasn't going to keep her grandmother waiting any longer.

CHAPTER 44

"Grandma?" Jillian could hear the wavering in her own voice and hated herself for it. Grandma Lucy needed her to be strong. The ER doctor's initial assessment had been anything but promising. With all the fluid around Grandma Lucy's heart, he told the family to be prepared if she didn't survive the night. Connie and Uncle Dennis were out in the lobby calling in any of the relatives within driving distance to come say their goodbyes.

Jillian still couldn't believe it. People like Grandma Lucy didn't die. Or if they did, their deaths were quick and painless and peaceful, not long, drawn-out battles in hospital rooms.

Jillian took a few tentative steps toward the bedside. "Grandma?" she repeated.

Her grandmother blinked at her. How could a woman as timeless as Grandma Lucy age two decades in one evening?

Jillian sniffed. If she hadn't been so stupid, she wouldn't have blabbed everything about the pregnancy to Ricky on the way here. She needed all her emotional strength just to get through the next few minutes.

She wasn't ready. She would never be ready. Not for this.

She picked up Grandma Lucy's hand. Where was the strength in her grip? Where was the warmth that always emanated from her touch?

"Can you hear me?" Jillian asked in such a small voice she could hardly hear herself.

Grandma Lucy nodded faintly. Her white hair lay in matted clumps against the colorless pillowcase. Jillian had never been one who craved physical affection. So why did she wish to curl up on Grandma Lucy's bed and wrap the old woman in one last hug?

Then again, Grandma Lucy looked so frail and weak Jillian was afraid that if she so much as sneezed she might blow the last breath out of her at any moment.

"I'm sorry," she whispered, squeezing Grandma Lucy's hand. "I'm so sorry. There's so much more I wanted to tell you." She sniffed and ignored the tears that streaked down her cheeks. She knew she must look like a mess and probably smelled even worse after spending the past hour in the barn with the silly goat who thought she was a puppy, but what did her appearance matter? Ricky was the only person she knew besides family here, and she was certain that after what she told him in the car, she had permanently cured him of any misplaced crush he had on her.

She looked down at her grandmother. How could a woman whose soul was so strong and powerful look this tiny, like a handheld fan could blow her away?

She hated the feel of Grandma Lucy's limp, lifeless hand. "I don't know what I'm supposed to say," she admitted. "I guess I want you to know how thankful I am that you've always been there for me. Even today, you prayed for me instead of judging me for what I've gone through. I wish ..." She sniffed and glanced around the room to see if there were any tissues. "I wish more Christians could be like you. It's hard, you know. I've blamed God for the way the people here treated my family and me. Honestly, my spiritual life hasn't been the same since then, but I look at you, and I think about how strong your faith is, and I'm ashamed that I didn't live up to your expectations."

Tears continued to pour down her face. She clenched

her throat shut for a moment, refusing to let out a cry but unable to say any more until she had composed herself.

"I guess, if there's one thing I want to tell you, it's about how I … It's that when I … Oh, never mind."

It had only been a few minutes ago when she convinced herself that she needed to come clean and confess everything to her grandmother, but now she knew she couldn't. What would be the point?

Telling Ricky certainly hadn't purged her soul from her guilt or made her feel any better.

She should go. Help Aunt Connie make some of those calls or something. Anything to get out of this room where the sorrow and the grief and the despair threatened to consume her entirely.

She turned to go but stopped when she heard her grandmother take in a wheezy breath of air.

"Did you say something?" Jillian's heart was fluttering erratically. Why did she feel like the only thing she wanted to do was run away? Why did she feel like she was the one suffocating?

"Blessing," Grandma Lucy whispered hoarsely.

Jillian leaned over the bedside. "What did you say? What do you mean?" She held Grandma Lucy's hand once more, terrified God might take her home before she told

Jillian what she was trying to say.

"Your baby will be a blessing." Each word seemed to drain more of the color out of Grandma Lucy's pale face, and when she was done, she retreated even deeper into her pillow. Into her weakness.

Jillian bowed her head as her tears dripped onto Grandma Lucy's face full of familiar laugh lines, tiny tributaries of joy.

"I told you, Grandma. Don't you remember? The baby didn't make it."

Any relief Jillian had once felt to hear that she would no longer have to carry her child to term paled next to the grief she felt at the thought of God taking her grandmother away from her.

Lord, don't you know I still need her here? Who will pray for me once she's gone?

"Your child is blessed," Grandma Lucy muttered. Her eyelids fluttered, closed, and then all was silent and still.

CHAPTER 45

Ricky had already ignored three calls from his mother. When his work cell rang, Ricky knew he had to pick up.

"Hi, Dad."

"Your mother's worried about you," his father said in lieu of a more conventional greeting.

"Tell her I'm fine. I'm here at the hospital with Jillian." Not technically a lie, even though Jillian had been back in Grandma Lucy's room for nearly half an hour while Ricky was stuck out here in the waiting room, wondering what he should do next.

"You best come home now, son."

"I know, but tell Mom I'll wait a little bit more until I get another update on Grandma Lucy. Then I'll be back."

A growl from his stomach reminded him he'd left the house without any dinner. He knew his father was right. Jillian was at the hospital. She was with her grandmother, and Connie and Dennis were here too if she needed anything. There was nothing more Ricky could do to help.

From the other end of the line, he heard his mother's nagging in the background.

"You tell him yourself," his father grumbled.

Ricky couldn't hear Mom's response but could sense the resentment in her tone.

His father sighed. "Your mother wants me to tell you to remember what she said about that girl. I assume you know what she's talking about."

"Yeah," Ricky sighed. "I do."

He was beginning to grow more and more thankful that Jillian had shut him down when she did. Even if they had anything in common, which they apparently didn't, how could he expect to develop any sort of relationship with someone his own mother would refuse to acknowledge?

He heard his father open a door. There was silence until it clicked shut behind him. "There's one more thing I want to tell you."

Where was he? His office?

"Out in a minute!" His father called then lowered his voice. "Now, son, it's time we had a talk."

Great. Had his father heard about the failed date at Olive Garden?

"It's about Grandma Lucy."

Ricky blinked and stared at his lap, surprised to see that both his legs were perfectly still.

"She's not right in the head. You know that, don't you? Your mother told me about church on Sunday, and religion's just fine to a degree, but like everything else, you've got to take it in moderation. Not like Grandma Lucy. Understand what I'm saying?"

No, Ricky didn't understand. He waited for his father to continue.

"It's like this. As men, we need to be willing to be the spiritual heads of our homes. Show up for church, lead prayers at the dinner table. But we also have other responsibilities that are just as important. Provide for our families, lead respectable lives in our community."

Ricky clenched and unclenched his fists.

"Christianity in excess is fine if you're an eccentric old lady like Lucy, but a boy like you, a boy who's one day going to inherit his father's business, has a lot more important things to think about. That's a lesson I don't ever want you to forget, son. Do you understand me?

"Yes, sir," Ricky replied automatically. "I understand."

He understood, but that didn't mean he agreed.

"So you come home now so your mother stops

worrying about you. Got that?"

Ricky thought carefully about what he was going to say next. He could tell his father exactly what he wanted to hear, leave the hospital, and fill his empty belly.

Or he could stay here, waiting for a young woman who probably didn't need him and certainly wouldn't appreciate his presence.

Ricky licked his lips, cleared his throat, and managed to reply, "I think I'll stick around a little longer. Tell Mom not to bother holding dinner."

CHAPTER 46

Ricky didn't realize until now that it was possible to twiddle your thumbs until the muscles got sore. Still no word from Jillian. Connie and Dennis were back there too. He wondered how long he should make a fool of himself by waiting here. The longer he sat around, the more awkward it would be when Jillian came out and let him know he wasn't needed.

What a waste of time.

He glanced up when he heard the lobby entrance open, and two women he recognized from church walked through. Jumping to his feet, he hurried toward them.

"Hi, Mrs. Porter. Mrs. Shin."

They frowned at him in turn. "Ricky, what's the matter?"

"Is your mother ill?"

He shook his head. "No, it's Grandma Lucy. She's here

sick, and …"

The two women exchanged meaningful glances. Great. Did that mean the entire town of Orchard Grove knew about his and Jillian's date?

"And how is Grandma Lucy?" Mrs. Porter asked.

He shuffled his weight from one foot to the other. "She's okay. I mean, I don't know that actually, but they haven't told me she's not okay, so hopefully she's doing all right."

The two women raised their eyebrows then walked to the window to talk to the receptionist. Ricky searched his pockets to make sure he wasn't leaving anything here. He had to go home, if for no other reason than that he was starving.

He'd call Jillian in the morning.

Maybe.

She'd told him a lot in the truck. Shared much more than he expected anybody to ever trust him with.

Maybe he should stay. That girl needed a friend.

Or maybe he should go.

He glanced at the time. *Give it five more minutes.*

He sat down again and picked up a magazine so it at least looked like he was occupied.

Mrs. Porter and Mrs. Shin took seats by the door. He'd

learned to tune out gossipy banter like theirs early on from all his mom's tea get-togethers with her lady friends, but he was snapped to alertness when he heard them say something about *that McAllister girl.*

"She's pregnant, you know."

"Heaven knows the world doesn't need another single mom on welfare."

"It's a pity. She was a very sweet little girl back in the day, wasn't she? So well behaved."

"I always thought there was something off about that family."

"I did too, but you know, there was something innocent about Jillian at the time."

A snort. "Innocence doesn't last long anymore, does it? You know, she wasn't even ..."

Ricky was on his feet before he knew what he was doing or where he was going. Even worse, his mouth was speaking before his brain had any idea what he planned to say.

"I'll have you two ladies know something. It's not Jillian's fault that she got pregnant. And if it weren't for old gossips like the two of you, she ..." It was at this moment his mind caught up to his tongue, and he balked at his own brazenness. The two women stared at him with eyes as wide as their mouths, but he didn't stop. "She's a sad, lonely young woman because people like you have taught her that Christians are all hypocritical, judgmental ..." He struggled to find the right words and ended up simply moving on before he lost his momentum. "So it's easy for you to sit there and talk bad about her, but you don't know what she's been through, how much she's been hurt and used and mistreated, and ..."

Mrs. Porter shook her head at him. "Does your mother know you're here?"

"Why? We're not talking about my mother. We're talking about Jillian McAllister. Not *that McAllister girl.* She has a name, she has a history, she has a past full of hurts that the two of you wouldn't even ... That you don't know the half of, and ..." He was doing it again. Speaking so fast he lost track of what he was trying to say.

He clenched his sweaty palms and finally muttered, "I guess that's all. I'll see you later."

Without waiting for the chastisement he knew would come if he hesitated any longer, he turned toward the door while one of the women muttered, "See? That girl will corrupt all the young men in this town if she stays here."

Ricky paused with his hand on the door. *Just walk on out,* he told himself. *Walk on out.*

His pickup was less than twenty feet away. He could see the dashboard from here.

Just walk on out, he repeated.

The women were muttering behind his back.

"What do you expect from a girl who gets herself pregnant like that?"

Nope, he wasn't going to heed his own advice.

What did it matter? His mom would hear about his outburst whether he pressed the issue further or not.

So what did he have to lose?

He spun on his heel and in three strides was towering over the women. From their surprised faces, you'd think they had forgotten he was an adult now, not the little five-year-old he'd been when they taught his Sunday school class.

"There's something the two of you should know before you go around spreading any more gossip like that, which I'm told by the way is a sin if you read your Bible carefully. Jillian didn't go out and *get herself pregnant* like you said. She was raped, okay? Some crazy ex-boyfriend who wouldn't leave her alone. So yeah, that changes things, doesn't it? Maybe from now on when you're getting your kicks out of spreading rumors like that just because you're self-centered, judgmental, bitter old ..." Where was the word he was looking for? Why couldn't he ever say what he really wanted?

He was breathing fast. His doctors had told him years ago he'd outgrown his asthma. Why this tightening now in his chest?

"And that's all I have to say," he concluded, accentuating his closing statement with a firm nod of the head.

"Ricky?" The voice was so soft, so low he didn't recognize it.

He whipped his head around quickly enough that the movement made him dizzy. Mrs. Shin and Mrs. Porter vanished from his line of sight. It was just the same as if they'd never stepped foot into County Hospital a day in their lives.

"Jillian?"

There was something different in her face. She usually looked so confident. Hard.

What were those black lines down her cheeks? Had something happened to her makeup?

Why did she look so little? He thought she was taller.

He hurried toward her, his only desire to protect her from all that pain and heaviness he saw in her expression. After years spent trying to figure out a woman's nonverbal cues, here was someone he could actually read.

"Jillian." Could she tell how glad he was to see her? How long he'd been waiting for her, worrying about her? "How is your grandma? Is she going to make it? Please tell me she's not already ..."

Something stung his face. What was that? He rubbed his cheek. What happened?

He blinked at her, unable to comprehend how this woman he felt so protective towards could have caused him that sort of pain. "What is it?" he asked, trying to figure out if he'd said something wrong.

Was she mad he hadn't come back to be with her? The receptionist told him the room was for family only.

"How could you?" she hissed so low he had to bend down to hear her. His face was so close to hers he could have nuzzled her nose if he wanted.

Which he didn't. Not now, at least, with her glaring like that after she slapped him.

"What's wrong?"

She shook her head and made her voice even lower. "You promised you wouldn't tell anyone. What were you thinking?"

CHAPTER 47

"Listen, I'm sorry." Ricky had lost track of how many times he'd apologized since he convinced Jillian to talk things through. He got the feeling that she only agreed to sit out here in his pickup with him to avoid a confrontation with Mrs. Porter and Mrs. Shin in the lobby, but it was a start.

He had to make her understand. "I was trying to defend you."

"By telling them what happened to me? Even after you promised not to?"

He cringed at her onslaught, wondering how a woman who just a minute earlier had looked so helpless and defenseless could be so angry.

"They were talking about you." Why didn't she understand? Out of everyone, she should know what people here at Orchard Grove were like. Sometimes the truth is the only thing that would shut up these stupid old gossips.

"Do you think I care if they were talking about me or not? Do you think it's any of their business how I got pregnant? That's exactly why I didn't tell anyone about what happened to begin with. Because the girls always get blamed. I guarantee you that they're in there right now speculating about what I was wearing or whether or not I'd been drinking when it happened or if it isn't my fault since I was stupid enough to date that idiot in the first place."

She shook her head. "You really did it, didn't you? I have no idea why I told you. For some stupid, crazy reason, I got it in my mind that you were someone I could trust ..."

"You can trust me," he pleaded. He hated how whiney he sounded, but what could he do?

How had everything turned out so backwards?

"Don't even talk to me."

How he was supposed to do that when she was still sitting next to him in his parked pickup? Did she just want him to leave so she could have some privacy? Maybe he would, but that would mean going back into that lobby, facing those two women himself ...

His mind already echoed with the sounds of all his mother's threats and lectures.

What had he been thinking?

For some insane reason, he'd expected her to be glad that he'd rushed to her defense. How stupid could a guy be?

He let out his breath. If she didn't want to talk, that was fine, but he still had to figure out how he was supposed to get himself home when she was sitting here in the front of his ...

"Oh."

At first he thought it was another round of her angry outbursts, but something was different. Something was wrong.

"You okay?"

She looked like she was in pain, but he resisted the urge to reach out and touch her shoulder. Make some kind of physical connection. He'd done enough damage for one night. He could see that now.

She squeezed her eyes shut and gripped her midsection. "Oh," she repeated.

He felt his eyes widen. "Holy cow. Did your water just break?"

"No, you idiot. I'm having a miscarriage." She let out another groan.

Were miscarriages supposed to hurt? How should he know?

"What do we do? Do you need to see the doctor? I could drive you to the hospital."

"We're at the hospital." Her teeth were clenched, and she reached out to grab onto her door handle. "This is terrible."

"Tell me what to do. Should I get you some hot water? Do you need any clean rags?"

"Will you shut up?"

This time, he was relieved to obey. Except now he didn't know what he was supposed to do with all that extra nervous energy.

She reached out and slapped his knee. "Stop jostling the car like that." She grabbed her forehead and groaned again.

"Something's wrong. We've got to get you to the doctor."

"I already saw the doctor this morning. He told me this would happen. The baby hasn't passed yet."

"Wait, I thought this was a miscarriage. You mean there's a real live baby in there?" A bead of sweat trickled down his temple.

"It's dead, stupid. That's why they call it a miscarriage."

"Maybe there's something we can do to save it …"

She shook her head. "For the love of everything holy in the entire universe, will you do me the biggest favor of my life and stop talking?"

CHAPTER 48

Jillian would never trust a male OB-GYN again, not for as long as she lived.

Dr. Morrison had told her she'd feel *moderate cramping* and that was it. Nothing to prepare her for the way her entire abdomen would seize itself shut without warning.

Or that the fire in her back from the contractions radiated outward.

"Do you need to see the doctor?"

How many times had Ricky asked her that in the past two minutes? She ignored him, focusing instead on not passing out from the pain.

If this was even a fraction of what labor might be like, she would never let another man touch her for as long as she lived.

If only her mom were here with her. Even through the pain, Jillian could still recognize the irony. Here she was, miscarrying the child her mother had been so ashamed of, and now Jillian would give just about anything for her mom to be the one sitting here beside her, not some hillbilly country boy who tripped over his own feet as often as his words.

She didn't know how bad the bleeding was yet, but she had an extra pad in her purse. Every fiber of her body wanted to go home to Aunt Connie's, throw on her pajamas, and bury herself under those soft prayer quilts. But what about her grandmother?

The ER doctor said if Grandma Lucy survived the night, she might make it after all. But it would still be touch and go for a few days, and the family had to be ready at a moment's notice to say their goodbyes. Aunt Connie and Uncle Dennis had been on the phone with the relatives all night long.

Jillian hadn't heard from her own parents yet, but maybe they'd be coming.

Maybe Jillian could have her mom by her side after all.

She wasn't ready for any of this.

She pulled out her phone.

"What are you doing?" Ricky asked.

The truth was she didn't know. Was she seriously naïve enough to expect that a phone call home would take away her problems instead of causing more?

She opened up her cell's browser. "I just want to look up what you're supposed to do when you're having a miscarriage."

"Oh. I can help. You just tell me what you need."

She ignored his eager-beaver comment and scrolled through the first few sites that popped up. Forums, blog posts, more medical stats. According to most of the experts, she was early enough in the pregnancy she should be able to get through everything without many problems, but those were probably the same people like Dr. Morrison who told her all she needed to expect was some *moderate cramping.*

Tears stung her eyes, but she didn't know why. She should be relieved. She hadn't wanted this child in the first place. And Grandma Lucy was at least a little more stable than she'd been when Jillian first arrived. It had been perfect timing for Ricky to show up when he did to drive her over here. What if she'd started cramping like this when she was all alone at the farm house?

"I need to use the bathroom."

Ricky stared at her as if she'd just confessed that she enjoyed eating kittens for breakfast. "I don't have anything in here that would work ..."

"Just unlock the door and let me out."

"Oh. Okay." He didn't take his eyes off her. "Are you sure you want to go in there? With those two women, I mean?"

She had bigger things to worry about than two old gossips. "Let them think what they want."

"I'm really sorry I said what I did. I shouldn't have ever let anyone else know."

She shrugged. "Doesn't matter now." She'd already come to realize that as long as she remained in Orchard Grove, there wasn't a single part of her life that would remain private. That's why she was so eager to get back to Seattle.

Just as soon as Grandma Lucy recovered.

She had to recover ...

She let herself out of his truck, and before Ricky could jump out and open her door for her, she was on the curb, making her way one unsteady step at a time to the County Hospital entrance.

CHAPTER 49

"Ricky? Is that you?" His mother's screeching voice pierced through the chaos of his thoughts. "What in the world kept you out so late? Do you have any idea what time it is?"

He glanced up, too drained to even make eye contact. "Hi, Mom."

"*Hi, Mom*? You storm out of here like some petulant teenager and come home at some ungodly hour, you've got the whole church worked up by the way you treated two of my closest friends, and all you can say is *hi, Mom*?"

It didn't matter how old he got. In his mother's eyes, Ricky had no reason to be out of the house past eight o'clock at night. Ever.

"I'm going to bed," he muttered. It had been an exhausting night, first worrying about Grandma Lucy and then with Jillian and her miscarriage ...

"Oh, no you're not, young man."

"I said I'm going to bed," he repeated. His stomach growled, but he hoped his mom wouldn't hear.

Mom jutted out her hip, narrowed her eyes, and crossed her arms. "You listen to me. Your father and I want to have a word with you."

"Leave the boy alone," his dad hollered from his office. "I've got him working double shifts the next two days, so let him get some sleep for crying out loud."

Mom huffed. "Well, fine, but tomorrow when you come home from work ..."

Ricky shuffled past her. "Yeah, yeah, I know. We'll talk then."

Upstairs in his room, he changed his clothes, which still smelled like the Safe Anchorage Goat Farm. Had it really just been this evening he'd gone over to find Jillian sitting with Peaches' head in her lap?

He couldn't remember the last time he felt so exhausted. He just hoped Jillian was all right.

After she got out his truck, he'd followed her back into the hospital. He wanted to be there in case Mrs. Porter or Mrs. Shin decided to give her a hard time, but they were quite skilled at avoiding all eye contact and doing their best to blend into the wall when he and Jillian entered the lobby. Connie was there, and Jillian must have explained what was going on, because Connie had a hushed conversation with the nurse, thanked Ricky for taking such good care of her niece, and hustled Jillian into the back room.

He just hoped that whatever was happening to her wasn't that bad. He knew nothing about miscarriages but made the mistake of googling some of the things to look out for. Hemorrhaging, infection ... He might have stayed at the hospital later, but he couldn't stand the thought of sitting in that lobby with those two old women, so he came back home.

Back to the lecture he knew was coming. At least it could wait until tomorrow.

He'd made a big mistake. Jillian had trusted him with her secret, and now the whole town knew.

He thought that if he explained what really happened, people like Mrs. Porter and Mrs. Shin would leave poor Jillian alone, but she was right. All he'd done was given them more cause for speculation, more sins to accuse her of.

Maybe Jillian had the right idea after all.

Maybe it was time to get out of Orchard Grove.

CHAPTER 50

"Now, you just lie down and ring this bell if you need anything, and I'll come here in a jiffy."

Jillian did her best to smile. Connie had been doting over her all night. Her aunt was so distraught at the news of the miscarriage, she could hardly drive home.

"I'm just so sorry this is happening, hon. I feel like it's all my fault. Do you think it's something you ate?"

Jillian could hardly pay attention. The cramping was so bad each peak sent waves of nausea cascading through her entire system. Connie could go ahead and mourn the baby who would never be.

Jillian was just trying to survive the miscarriage itself.

"You should be back with Grandma Lucy," she told her aunt, who insisted on tucking her in beneath the prayer quilts as if Jillian had been a little toddler.

Connie shook his head. "Your uncle will call me if anything changes, and that's all we can ask for in times like this. God's pulled Grandma Lucy through worse scares than this, and if he wants to do it again, that's just what he'll do. You can mark my words. And as for you, get plenty of rest and make sure you're changing your pads as often as you need ..."

"I'm fine." Jillian hadn't meant to snap, but any more smothering and she swore she'd suffocate.

Connie leaned over and kissed her on the forehead. Was Jillian wearing some sort of invisible sign that said, *I'm needy and pathetic. Please baby me*?

Oh, well. She'd never admit it out loud, but maybe it was nice to be doted over.

At least every so often.

"Do you think that pain medicine the nurse gave you's kicked in yet?" Connie asked. "Because I can call the doctor and see if you can take another dose. It's a little early, but maybe you'll sleep better."

Jillian shook her head. "I'm doing all right." She couldn't even remember the name of the stuff they gave her back at County, but it must be working. At least she didn't feel like she was about to puke from the pain.

Connie swept some stray strands of hair out of Jillian's eyes. "I love you, sweetie. You know that, don't you?"

"I know."

She clutched Jillian's hand in hers. "And I'm so sorry about your little baby. I know you would have been a wonderful mother."

Jillian didn't bother to remind her aunt the child would have been put up for adoption.

She was too tired to talk or think about anything.

Connie muttered a few more soft pleasantries, but Jillian's brain was already starting to drift off into a dark and mercifully painless oblivion.

CHAPTER 51

True to his word, Ricky's father kept him working twelve-hour days so that by the time he finished his runs, there wasn't any time left to drive all the way out to Baxter Loop to check on things at Safe Anchorage. No word about Jillian or her family from his mom either, who usually loved to keep him abreast of all the Orchard Grove gossip.

All Ricky was able to find out by Friday evening was that Grandma Lucy had made it through her first night but still had a long recovery ahead of her. There was discussion about her moving into the Winter Grove assisted living home where she could get round-the-clock care, at least if she ever made it out of the hospital.

Ricky had no idea how Jillian was. He figured if something was drastically wrong, someone would have told him, or he would have overheard something somewhere. That's just the way Orchard Grove worked.

He tried to call her. Well, that wasn't actually the truth.

He'd taken out his phone and pulled up her number dozens of times, but he had no idea how to start that sort of conversation.

Hey, so tell me about the miscarriage. Was it as bad as it sounds?

It wasn't until Saturday morning after he dropped his mom off at the annual spring health fair that he found himself with a free hour.

Baxter Loop, here I come.

It had rained recently, making the potholes on the long gravel road even worse to maneuver than normal. At least he was in his mom's car this time and not the pickup.

He was so jittery he felt like he'd just downed three energy drinks. What if Jillian wasn't happy to see him? What if she didn't forgive him for telling those two women (and by extension everyone else in Orchard Grove) what really happened to her? What if the sight of him did nothing but remind her of that terrible night in the hospital?

He shouldn't even be here.

But he wasn't going to turn around. Anything was better than not knowing. If Jillian told him to get lost, if she said she never wanted to see him again, he could live with that.

What he couldn't live with was wondering each day

how she was feeling. If she'd recovered from everything she went through.

If she hated him for disclosing her secret.

If she was still just as lonely and hurting and lost as she seemed when she first moved back to Orchard Grove.

He pulled into the long Safe Anchorage driveway as a tiny goat kid bounced up onto a plastic tub and back down.

Connie was smiling, taking pictures of the newborn with an old-fashioned disposable camera. The goat had a pinkish tint to its coat.

"Is that Peaches' baby?" Ricky asked when he got out of the car.

Connie nodded. "Delivered yesterday morning, and just the cutest little thing, isn't he?"

Ricky reached down to pet the inquisitive creature and asked, "How's Grandma Lucy?"

"Getting more of her strength back every day."

"Will she be coming home soon, then?"

"No. Doctors think it will be a while yet. And we're still considering if it's time for her to move into Winter Grove. I hate to think of her all alone there, but of course, it's not that far, and we could visit every day and even bring her back to the farm couple hours at a time to meet the babies." She sighed heavily. "Dennis is over at the hospital now. She's sleeping most of the time, but every so often she wakes up. You know Grandma Lucy. Her spirit's strong as ever."

As much as he might like to pretend he had nothing better to do than to chat with Connie and pet her newest little member of the herd, that wasn't why he drove all the way out here. Ricky met Connie's gaze head-on. "Where's Jillian? I wanted to talk to her."

Connie frowned. "You mean she didn't call? That girl. She promised she would let you know."

Ricky stared at the baby goat, who was nibbling at his jeans. "Let me know what?"

Connie shook her head. "Maybe she tried to text. You know, sometimes those messages can just get lost, and there's no guessing where they end up. Probably up there with the satellites or stuck in the Internet somewhere so you'll never find them again."

"Tell me what?" he repeated.

Connie let out her breath. "I'm sorry, hon. It's nothing personal against you, I'm sure, but Jillian went home. She's back in Seattle."

.

CHAPTER 52

"Jillian, we're leaving in five minutes."

Jillian glanced at her reflection in the mirror. After moving back home, everything reverted to exactly how it had been. Saturday evening setting the chairs up in the high-school gym where they'd meet for services Sunday morning. Monday night prayer meetings. Tuesday night Bible study.

It's amazing how one little miscarriage can turn everything back to normal.

Well, just about everything. Next week, she'd start working at her uncle Joseph's office, and she'd save up enough money to move into the dorms by fall. She hadn't told her parents about the ultimate end goal. She hated to break it to them now with her brother missing for the past two weeks, undoubtedly out on another drug binge. They didn't need to know about where she'd be living next semester.

Besides, they'd find out soon enough.

Her phone dinged at her. A text from Ricky. She'd known it would just be a matter of days. She was surprised she hadn't heard from him sooner.

Surprised and perhaps a tad disappointed. Not that she'd admit it to anyone besides herself.

Maybe she should have given him the courtesy of a proper goodbye, but you could hardly blame her under the circumstances. Whatever textbooks Dr. Morrison was reading, he'd really have to work on his definition of *moderate cramping* when telling his patients what to expect during a miscarriage.

The worst of it was over now, though, thank God. And just like that she was accepted at home again.

Why had she been so eager to return to Seattle?

She thought she'd feel more relieved. She thought she'd feel grateful to be back.

It wasn't the first time she'd been wrong.

She ignored Ricky's text. What good would it serve to stay in touch with someone she'd never see again? If she ever went back to Orchard Grove, it would be to visit Grandma Lucy, and that was it. Ricky Fields was now just a bad memory in her past, like everything else in Orchard

Grove

"Jillian, you ready?"

She took a deep breath and called down, "I'm on my way." Then she turned off her phone.

CHAPTER 53

She'd only spent one Sunday stuck away in Orchard Grove, but within her first few minutes back at her father's church in Seattle she sensed how much had changed.

People who two weeks ago had been cool or reserved now gave her heart-felt hugs, asking her how her week away visiting her grandmother was.

Ironic that Jillian went to Orchard Grove ostensibly to care for her aging grandmother, and now that Grandma Lucy was in the hospital, Jillian was back home.

Her mom pinched her elbow. "Stop scowling. You look miserable."

"I wasn't scowling," she muttered, but her mom had already sidled up to one of the new couples and ignored her.

Jillian sighed. Her dad's church catered to young families. Lots of toddlers running around, babies crying everywhere you turned. There were some teens here, but Jillian was too old for the youth group. Did she have any real friends here?

And why hadn't she realized before how there weren't any single women her age in this entire congregation?

She pulled out her phone. She hadn't even read Ricky's text yet. Why was she thinking about him now of all times? She glanced at her screen.

"Honey." Her mom pulled her arm. "Come here. There's a new family I want you to meet."

She shoved her phone back into her purse, wondering if she'd ever get around to sending Ricky a reply. What could she say?

She'd been so rude to him the last night they saw each other, and then she'd left Orchard Grove without telling him goodbye.

And that was it.

Jillian smiled her way through the introductions and greetings, but her mind was elsewhere. Listening to the boisterous laughter, the loud chats while people mingled together before the service started. Five dozen conversations reverberating in the open gym like individual swarms of mosquitoes except even louder and more annoying.

She glanced around at the fancy clothes, the glued-on smiles. Did anyone here know she'd just lost a baby? That it was hard to say whether she felt more guilty or relieved at any given moment? Did they care that her grandmother was in a hospital and might never leave?

Jillian had never felt so alone.

CHAPTER 54

Ricky wasn't sure what he'd been expecting out of today's service, but whatever it was, he hadn't found it.

It wasn't the preaching. Pastor Greg was a good speaker. He told memorable stories and kept the congregation's interest. So what was missing?

Maybe it was because Grandma Lucy wasn't there. But that couldn't be right. He should be able to worship God, to connect with the Lord, without the help of some little old granny lady, right?

At least she was continuing to recover. Connie's update during the prayer and praises part of the service was even more encouraging than it had been yesterday when he stopped by Safe Anchorage. If Grandma Lucy continued to show improvement and regained her strength, she'd be out of the hospital by the end of the week. The only question was whether she'd be headed back home or moving into

Winter Grove.

Part of Ricky hated to think of a woman as full of life and energy as Grandma Lucy spending her last days at an assisted living home, but maybe it would be for the best. Connie wasn't young anymore, and their old farmhouse with all its stairs and different levels was no place for a woman who might always need a wheelchair or at least a walker from now on.

For now, he didn't have time to think about it. His dad was expecting him at the office as soon as the service ended. He didn't say why, but Ricky wondered if this was finally the time when he'd be punished for telling Mrs. Porter and Mrs. Shin off in the hospital lobby, a conversation he was surprised hadn't happened last week.

Once church ended, he drove Mom home while listening to her numerous critiques of the preaching, the music, and the attire of half of her friends in the Women's Missionary League. He dropped her off, then headed to work. He wasn't exactly sure what to expect but found himself praying for God to protect him from whatever might happen at this meeting with his dad.

He stepped into the office building tentatively, mentally preparing himself for the lecture that was sure to come. The problem was he didn't know if it had to do with his performance on the job, his outburst the other night at the hospital, or something else entirely.

His dad was finishing up a phone call and beckoned him in. Ricky stood over his father's desk, careful not to knock anything out of place, until his dad impatiently waved his hand, telling him to take a seat.

Dad ended the call, and Ricky grabbed a fistful of fabric from his pants in an attempt to keep his leg from bouncing.

"Have a seat," his dad said, and Ricky stared at his lap, wondering how he could sit down twice.

"I want to talk to you, son."

Ricky donned what he hoped was a humble expression, reminding himself that he was an adult now. He didn't have to be this nervous.

"You worked hard this week. Lots of extra hours."

Ricky nodded. It had been tiring, but at least it gave him an excuse to avoid his mother as much as possible. He wasn't going to complain about that.

"You're getting older now," his dad went on. "You're an adult. Ready for more responsibility, don't you think?"

Ricky knew it. This was the part when his dad would tell him that a man of Ricky's age and position in the community had no business yelling at little church ladies in the emergency room lobby. He was already formulating the beginnings of his apology when his dad went on, "Your mother and I talked it over, and we both agree. It's time to move you up to a manager position."

Ricky blinked. His leg stopped jumping. He swallowed down the apology he was planning to stammer. "Huh?"

"A promotion. I want you to be one of my managers. Think you're ready for that?"

Ricky nodded. "Yes, sir."

"Good." His dad shuffled some papers on his desk. "But before we make things official, there's one small catch."

Ricky gulped. Here it was. Well, whatever his dad wanted to say, he may as well get it out in the open. Anything was better than uncertainty.

Ricky listened while his father spelled out his terms, the beginnings of a sly smile creeping up the corners of his lips. "Are those terms acceptable?"

For once in his life, Ricky knew exactly what he had to do. There was no hesitating. "Yes, sir. I accept your terms."

CHAPTER 55

Two months later

Jillian was exhausted. At least her uncle Joseph's office had air conditioning, but she was still sweltering after braving the Seattle summer heat to grab a burrito from the little taco stand across the street.

She'd have indigestion for the rest of the afternoon, but the extra sour cream and onions were worth every second of discomfort.

She glanced at the clock. She had to leave half an hour early today for her doctor's appointment.

"Jillian, could you go get these ready to go out in tomorrow's mail?" her supervisor, Misty, asked.

Jillian nodded, even though she had just sat down and hated the idea of getting back on her feet again.

Oh, well. Working for her uncle Joseph was far less

physically demanding than any other job she could think of, and the pay was more than she could find at most retailers or restaurants. She wouldn't complain.

By fall, just like she planned, she'd have enough money to afford an apartment off campus. For now, she was living with a couple connected to the pregnancy center she'd visited so many months ago. It wasn't perfect. They had a nine-month-old who screamed at all hours of the night — her mom claimed teething, but Jillian was beginning to wonder if their child had just been cursed with a terrible personality — but it was still better than the drama at home.

Every once in a while, she asked herself if she'd done the right thing returning to Seattle. Grandma Lucy was home now at Safe Anchorage, but she couldn't get around anymore without her walker and even had a wheelchair to use when she was especially tired.

Sometimes Jillian felt guilty about the way she left, especially how she never said goodbye to that Ricky fellow or responded to any of his texts. Thankfully, the poor soul gave up after just a few weeks. Although she had to give him some credit for his persistence.

"Can you drop these off downstairs when you close up?" Misty asked.

Jillian shook her head. "I'm leaving early, remember?

Doctor's appointment."

"Oh, yeah. How are you feeling, by the way?"

Jillian shrugged. "About as good as you can expect, I guess."

Misty nodded absently and headed into her office cubicle, high heels clicking behind her.

The intercom buzzed. "Courier delivery for Mr. Gregory."

She pushed a button on her headset. "Send him up."

She was in the middle of printing up invoices for her uncle when she heard a vase topple over. Someone was bending over it, trying to mop up the spilled water with the doily Misty had laid out on the end table.

"I'm so sorry," he stammered and then stopped when his eyes met hers.

"Jillian?"

"Ricky?" She felt her face heat up and blamed it on the burrito.

"What are you doing here?"

"You're in Seattle now."

They both spoke at once, and Ricky let out a chuckle. That was a good sign. At least he didn't hate her for skipping town without saying goodbye or ignoring him for the past two months.

"I'm working here now," he said. "My dad's been wanting to start up business here in Seattle, and he brought me on as one of his new managers."

"That's great. I, um, I hope you're having a good time so far."

He nodded. "Yeah, sorry about that vase, though."

"Don't mention it." She stood up to find some paper towels when she heard him gasp. "Whoa! Is that a baby in there?"

She stared at him.

He stood there clenching and unclenching his fists and rocking from side to side. "I mean, no, it's not that ... Maybe it's the shirt, you know, I ... I'm just going to shut up now." He sputtered as he turned to leave, but then glanced over his shoulder once more. "I'm sorry. You look good, it's just that ... Well, it's probably the shirt. Sorry again about the vase." He headed to the door and stopped one more time and hurried to her desk. "Whoops. I almost forgot. This is for you. Or your boss, I suppose, Mr. Gregory. I just need a signature here, and then I'll be gone. Nice running into you. And nice shirt too. It's, umm, very blue."

He was already to the door when she called after him. "Ricky, wait."

"Yeah?"

She wasn't ready to have this conversation from the other side of the office, so she grabbed some paper towels and made her way over toward him. "Since you're new to town, maybe you could use someone to show you around from time to time." She picked up the toppled vase and raised her eyes to his.

"Oh, that's really sweet, but I've got GPS in my car, so I think I'm fine." Ricky's eyes widened. "Oh. Maybe that's not what you meant." He was staring at her stomach, but she knew there were some things that would have to wait.

She took in a deep breath. "I have a doctor's appointment in a little while, and then I'm free for the rest of the night. Do you have any dinner plans?"

He ran his fingers through his hair. "Yeah, thanks. I just went to the store yesterday and got a whole week's worth of frozen pizzas, so I'm all set." He frowned at her. "Oh, wait. Were you asking ... Sorry. I'm just a little surprised seeing you here, I guess. Are you saying you want to get some dinner together? Like I said, I have some pizzas, but I have to warn you, my roommates are both slobs, and the apartment kinda smells like ..."

"What about Olive Garden?" she asked.

"Olive Garden?"

"Yeah. Ever heard of it?"

His nervous jittering calmed down, and a smile — genuine this time — spread across his face.

"Yeah, I've heard of it. In fact, I hear they have these killer breadsticks."

CHAPTER 56

Ricky couldn't remember the last time he had felt so confused. He tore off a piece of breadstick and asked, "So you did or didn't have a miscarriage?"

Jillian gulped down a drink of ice water. "Well, I didn't know at the time, but I was pregnant with twins. So yes, I lost one, but his sister stayed strong and healthy throughout the miscarriage."

"So is it a boy or girl?" Ricky wasn't sure why Jillian stared at him so confused, but she finished off her glass of water and answered, "A girl."

"And you're ..." Ricky tried to figure out what he was trying to ask. "Are you going to be her mom?"

She furrowed her brow. "I already am her mom."

Ricky felt his face flush. Good thing Olive Garden kept their lights so dim. "I mean, are you going to keep her?" No, that didn't come out right. Isn't that what you say about stray cats or puppies?

"I found an adoptive family."

Ricky wasn't sure what the correct response was supposed to be. Did he say congratulations? When she didn't offer any more information, he figured he'd better stick to safer topics. "So, is it fun eating for two?"

Jillian let out a little laugh. From the first day he saw her back in Orchard Grove, Ricky realized he wanted little more than to keep on finding ways to make her smile.

She took her fourth breadstick from the basket. "I guess you can say it has its perks."

Neither one said anything, but the silence was comfortable. Ricky himself was quite impressed with the way he had gone through the meal so far without spilling anything on himself or his date.

Well, maybe this wasn't a date. Or was it? Yet another question that not even his Google searches seemed able to answer for him. Whatever it was, he didn't want it to end.

And he hoped there would be many, many more to come.

CHAPTER 57

Three and a half months later

"Where have you been?" Ricky's mom snapped. "Your father and I have been trying to get a hold of you for hours."

Ricky glanced at his phone, where he'd received one text from his dad about twenty minutes ago.

"Where are you at?" Mom demanded.

"I'm at the hospital. Jillian had her baby."

His mom made a snorting sound from the back of her throat. "Well then, I expect now that she's out of the hospital and not lying around doing nothing ..."

"She was on bedrest, Mom," Ricky interrupted.

"Well, whatever she was doing there, now that the child's out, I suspect you have better things to do with your time than spend heaven only knows how many hours a week courting that kind of a girl. You have more important matters to focus on, like …"

"Mom," he butted in again, "I already told you we're not breaking up." He shoved his hand into his pocket. "We've got something really special between us."

"Yeah," she snorted. "Hormones."

"Mom," he whined.

"Well, I'm just naming it as I see it. You know that if you let things get any more serious with that girl, it's not going to lead to anything but more heartache for you and everyone else involved."

Whatever that was supposed to mean.

"So she still decided to give up the kid?"

"Yeah." Ricky had spent countless hours by Jillian's side, watching her hold the baby she would soon hand over to someone else. Up until now, he'd thought of adoption as a quick, easy solution. He hadn't realized what an emotional struggle it would be. He hadn't been in the room during the delivery itself, but even standing outside the door he'd heard Jillian crying for the child that would only be hers for a few short hours.

If one good thing came out of her month on bedrest, it was that it had brought the two of them even closer together. Sadly, most of Jillian's friends from school were really busy, and eventually their visits tapered off until

Ricky was often the only person Jillian talked to besides her nurses in a given day. He knew things were sticky at home, so they didn't mention her parents much.

Or his.

But that hadn't stopped him from falling in love with her through each evening visit, each stolen lunch break when he came by to keep her company.

It sounded stupid when he admitted it to himself, but he was scared that they'd drift apart once she got discharged from the hospital, once she went back to working full time for her uncle and started those fall semester night classes she'd signed up for.

He still worried that the reason she decided she loved him too was because he was the only person who came by to see her. She didn't have any other choices while she was on bedrest. But after this last goodbye between her and her baby girl, she'd be as free as a bird.

Maybe that's why Mom sounded somewhat pleased when he told her about the delivery.

"I gotta go," he told his mom. "I'll see you next week at Grandma Lucy's birthday party."

Another snort. "A woman at that age shouldn't celebrate each passing year. It isn't natural."

Ricky ignored her comment and clenched his sweaty

palms. "Oh, is Dad there? I had a quick question for him."

"Yeah. Should I put him on speaker?"

That was the last thing Ricky needed. "No, just give him the phone. It's ..." He was about to say *it's about work* but there was no way to twist that into even a partial truth. "It's just a quick question." There. That was better.

His dad got on the line. "Yeah?"

Ricky cleared his throat. He needed to get this out. "So, um, maybe you heard me talking to Mom, but Jillian had her baby."

"Uh-huh." His father sounded distracted. If Ricky didn't get to the point, he would lose his courage or his father would start asking him about things at the Seattle office.

"And, well, you know what we talked about a few weeks ago? That thing?" Ricky's face was burning up just from the allusion.

"Yes."

Now he had his dad's full attention at least. He hopped from one leg to the other in the hospital hallway. "Well, I'm thinking about doing it."

"Now? Today?"

"I don't know. Maybe."

"Son, she just had a baby. She's probably pretty

emotional."

"I know, but ..." But what? How could he explain it? He stared at the bleached floor. "Yeah, maybe you're right."

"Give her a little time. Delivering a baby, putting her up for adoption, these are huge things that you don't snap back from right away."

"Okay." He unclenched his fist which had wrapped itself around a small box in his pocket. "Yeah. Yeah, you're right. Thanks, Dad."

Ricky ended the call and went back into Jillian's room, where she was preparing to say goodbye to the daughter she'd so recently delivered.

CHAPTER 58

Ricky rubbed Jillian's tense shoulders.

"I really can't do this," she sniffed while patting the baby's back.

He glanced at the doorway, where soon the adoptive parents would come in to take her daughter away.

"There's still time," he whispered. Once they started officially dating, he'd gone with her to as many of the adoption counseling sessions as he could. He knew Washington state laws so well he could recite them.

"That's not what I mean."

One of the counselors had warned Ricky that Jillian would be hard to console after the delivery, a combination of the hormones plus the emotional roller coaster she'd chosen.

And Ricky had thought adoption was a simple solution.

He kissed the top of her head. "You're doing such a

good job," he said. "And whatever you decide, you know that no one else gets to tell you what to do."

Another line he'd heard so often from the counselors he could recite it in his sleep.

Jillian wiped her puffy face and kept on patting her daughter's back. "I'm trying as hard as I can. I really am."

"And you're doing a perfect job."

What was happening? Was she changing her mind? How did she expect to take care of a newborn? They weren't ready for any of this.

"It won't work," she sobbed again.

Ricky's throat seized up. He was ready to support her in each and every decision she made, but ... raising a baby?

He cleared his throat and reminded himself that this was a decision nobody could make but her. "You know I'll love and support you no matter what you decide."

She glanced up at him through teary eyes. "Huh?"

"If you change your mind," he explained and adjusted his pants. The jewelry box in his pocket was digging into his thigh. "I'll do whatever I need to do. I'll get a second job, I'll flip burgers for the rest of my life, I'll ..."

He stopped when he saw how oddly she was staring at him, as if he'd just suggested they eat her daughter for breakfast instead of handing her over to the adoptive parents.

"What are you talking about?"

"The adoption," he explained. "If you've changed your mind ..."

She shook her head. "That's not it."

"Then why were you crying?"

She looked so cute with her hair all tangled and her T-shirt hanging lopsided on her shoulder like that. She gave a tiny chuckle and passed Emily to him. "I just meant I can't figure out how to burp her. Can you try? You always seem to do it so much better than I do."

CHAPTER 59

For as long as she lived, she would never stop crying.

Rivers of tears, endless streams flowing down her face.

Searing hot like lava. Burning her skin.

"It's the right thing," she whispered. "I know it is."

Ricky leaned over and kissed her forehead. She hated to think about how sweaty and gross she was after the delivery. She hadn't stepped foot out of this hospital in weeks. While she was stuck here on bedrest after her water broke six weeks too early, she'd sworn she'd be the happiest woman in the world when she finally got to step outside. Summer was over, and she'd missed all of it either working for her uncle or lying around here.

Thank God Ricky was here. She would have lost her mind completely if it weren't for his daily visits. Sometimes he'd curl up with her, and they'd watch movies until midnight, and he'd still stop by on his lunch breaks no matter how busy things got at work.

Half a year ago, she thought that getting raped and then kicked out of her parents' home was the worst kind of pain she'd ever have to live through. But she'd found at least some semblance of healing. Maybe it was how gently Ricky treated her. No matter how many times she started beating herself up for getting pregnant in the first place, he reminded her that it wasn't her fault.

And every time she felt guilty for being pregnant out of wedlock, he reminded her that pregnancy itself was no sin, and that she'd actually made the bravest choice given her circumstances, enduring the pregnancy and four weeks of bedrest for the sake of her daughter.

A daughter that in just a few minutes she'd hand over to someone else.

It wasn't that the Kims were bad people. Hannah and Simon were the godliest couple Jillian had ever met. Before moving to the States, they'd done mission work in Asia, top secret stuff that even now they couldn't talk about without using code words like *restricted access nations*. He now pastored a Korean-speaking church in Massachusetts, and Jillian knew with complete certainty and conviction that they would give her daughter a beautiful, happy life.

The funny thing is the Kims acted as if Jillian was the

one doing them the favor. They'd tried for years to get pregnant, but it turned out they both had health complications that made natural conception impossible. They loved little Emily just as much as Jillian did.

And they would be good to her.

And in just a few minutes, they were coming to take her away.

CHAPTER 60

Ricky clung to the nurse's call remote like a sailor would cling to the debris of a shipwreck.

Soon a nurse in Linus and Lucy scrubs bustled in. "Can I help you?" If she was surprised to see a grown man on the hospital bed with his girlfriend on his lap, sobbing into his shoulder, she was tactful enough not to show it.

He waited until she got a little closer so he didn't have to shout across the room. "It's been almost an hour," he whispered. "Do you think there's something wrong?"

The nurse looked at Jillian with a sympathetic expression. "This is totally normal. She's been through more than you or I could ever imagine. The best thing you can do right now is be strong for her, let her know that it's not always going to hurt so bad."

Jillian's whole body shuddered, and Ricky tightened his arms around her. The corner of the jewelry box had been digging into his skin for almost half an hour, but he didn't want to adjust his weight or stick his hand down into his pocket. Not right now.

The nurse glanced at the clock. "We have chaplains here. Do you think she'd like to talk to somebody? Or maybe a social worker?"

He rubbed Jillian's back. "Would you like that?"

She shook her head.

Wasn't there anything he could do?

The nurse sighed, and this time her sympathy seemed directed toward him. "You're doing a good job of comforting her."

He guessed she meant well, but he knew she was lying. If he was doing a good job, his girlfriend wouldn't have soaked through his flannel shirt with her tears.

"You just call me if you need a little break," she told Ricky, "and I'll be happy to sit with her a while."

He glanced at the clock, wondering how long tears could flow like this before they ran completely dry.

Another shudder ran down Jillian's spine. All he could do was hold her closer. Remind her he was still here.

He always would be.

CHAPTER 61

The adoption counselors had talked about *empty arm syndrome*, but for some reason Jillian hadn't realized they were talking about an actual physical sensation.

Awake or asleep or in that torturous in-between state, she felt the heaviness of her empty arms.

Arms that just days earlier had held the most beautiful little girl she would ever see in her entire life.

Why had she picked an adoptive family who lived so far away?

The Kims were great. Hannah and Simon sent pictures every day, but how long would they keep that up? He'd go back to pastoring that church, she'd get wrapped up in her duties as a new mom, and they'd forget all about her.

Just like little Emily would.

Just like she already had.

The worst part for Jillian was knowing that she'd made

the right choice. That if God were ever so cruel as to make her relive this same kind of torture and pain, she'd have to go through all that searing loss all over again.

How could anyone be expected to endure that kind of torment?

These were the kinds of questions she was dying to ask, but she couldn't broach the subject with her mom, who hadn't even come to meet Emily at the hospital.

Refused to look when Jillian offered to show her pictures.

Was Jillian seriously supposed to wake up and go to work and pretend like she'd never delivered a child? Never held her own flesh and blood in her arms and then passed her on to someone else, someone she barely knew?

There was nothing more unnatural. Not in the entire universe. Mothers weren't supposed to give up their children.

Ever.

Even her body was rebelling against her decision. She hadn't thought to ask the doctor at her postpartum checkup how long this painful engorgement would last, but she was so sore and swollen she couldn't even hold herself upright.

At first, she thought she'd go to work right away, but how could she? She couldn't even make it from the couch to the kitchen for a drink of water without breaking down into tears.

She'd lost track of how many times she'd held that phone in her hand, wanting to call her mom, beg for the chance to come home even if only for a few days. But what good would that do?

Ricky was a saint, just like she'd come to expect of him, but he was gone all day. He'd call while he was on the road to check up on her, but whenever they talked, she felt so much pressure to convince him she was fine because she knew how much he worried about her.

At least today was Friday. Tomorrow, they'd drive out together to Orchard Grove for Grandma Lucy's birthday party. She just hoped that maybe she'd get all her tears out on the trip there so she could be presentable for her relatives. Of course, by now the details were public knowledge in Orchard Grove. She'd been raped, miscarried a twin, carried the other to term, and given it up to some Korean-American couple living on the East Coast — the past nine months now neatly summarized in one short little blurb.

At least she'd be making the drive with Ricky and not her parents, who were too busy with church obligations to take the weekend off. After spending so much time together since he moved to Seattle, Ricky was the one person she felt completely comfortable with.

Like she could truly be herself.

Or maybe a better version of herself.

Ricky made her want to improve. Made her want to try harder to be as thoughtful and compassionate as he was. She knew she had a long way to go, but as long as he was here to keep on setting such a good example, maybe — just maybe — she'd find a way to become the kind of Christian her grandmother prayed she'd be.

The kind of Christian who would make Grandma Lucy proud.

CHAPTER 62

Ricky had been watching Jillian for the past several minutes before he finally announced his presence. "Fun party, huh?"

She jumped and turned around. "Don't sneak up on me like that." The sun was low on the horizon, lighting up her face and hair as it streamed in through the barn window. She was absolutely irresistible.

"Sorry. I didn't mean to scare you." He walked up to her. A week and a half after the delivery, she still had a swollen belly she tried to hide under a loose flowery blouse, but he could feel it when he stood behind and wrapped his arms around her. "Your hair smells good."

"That's probably the goats you're smelling," she joked.

He kissed the top of her head. "I love you. I hope you know that."

She looked up at him with a face that was perfectly

trusting.

Perfectly kissable.

"I know. I love you too."

Could she hear how hard his heart was thumping? Could she feel it pounding against her?

"So." He cleared his throat. Glanced over to the corner where Peaches was nursing her baby, who'd probably doubled in size since the last time he'd been here. He shoved his hand into his pocket. "Are you having a good time?" He licked his lips. That wasn't what he meant to say.

She nodded. "Yeah. It's still hard."

"It'll probably be hard for a while." Wow, that was real encouraging. Time to change the subject. "Grandma Lucy's looking good."

"Yeah, that walker doesn't really slow her down at all, does it?" She pulled her eyes away from him and stared out the barn window. In the course of a second, she had moved a thousand miles away.

He'd seen that look more often than not since she came home from the hospital. "What is it?"

"I was just thinking of what Grandma Lucy said to me that night at the hospital. She said something about my baby being a blessing. I wish I could remember exactly what it was. But it was weird, because at that point we didn't know about Emily. We just knew about the miscarriage. But Grandma seemed so certain ..."

"That's Grandma Lucy for you."

"I know, but at the time I thought she was senile or something. Like she'd forgotten the baby was dead. But maybe she knew all along. I don't know. It sounds crazy."

This was his opening. He had to take it.

Shuffling his weight, he took her hand in his. For a second, he worried that he'd gross her out with his sweaty palms, but he had a lot more serious faults than that, and if she couldn't put up with them, she would have left by now.

"Speaking of Grandma Lucy," he began, "she said something interesting after lunch."

"Oh, yeah? I'll believe just about anything. What was it?"

"She said that she hopes God lets her live until at least next spring, and I asked why, and she said she didn't want to miss the wedding."

Jillian's eyes zoned in on his. "What wedding?"

"That's what I asked her. But then your aunt came up and said that they were about to blow out the candles on her cake, and she never told me the rest."

"Huh." Jillian was still staring at him. Still holding his

sweaty palm.

He shoved his free hand back into his pocket. "So, you know, speaking of things like weddings and stuff like that …" He kept his eyes locked on hers, wanting to make sure he was doing this at the right time.

"Yeah?"

"And maybe now that I think about it I should have written this all down or something because you know how hard it is for me when I get nervous and have to say something important."

Her eyes were soft, her expression patient. "You're doing fine."

"That's sweet of you to say, but I know I'm not." He ran his hands through his hair and licked his lips. When had they gotten so dry?

From the corner, Peaches let out a low moan and stamped her hoof as if she were as impatient with him as he was with himself.

"So, I've got something for you, and it's here in my pocket …" He tried to pry the box free, but it flew out of his hands and landed on a pile of hay beside him. He dropped to his knees and then realized he should have been in this position all along.

"Oh, no!"

ALANA TERRY

"What's wrong?" she asked.

"I lost it."

"The box? No, it's right there in your hand."

"Not the box." Still on the ground, Ricky held it open. "See, it's empty."

Just then, the barn door swung open, Connie glanced in with a little, "Oh," then hurried to shut the door again, calling out, "Don't mind me. I didn't see anything," while she sealed them back in.

Ricky was on all fours now, digging through the dirty hay. "I can't find it anywhere."

Jillian knelt beside him. "Let me help."

"But you don't know what we're looking for."

She smiled and kissed his cheek. "Maybe I'll recognize it when I see it."

This couldn't be happening. Of all the times for him to be so clumsy ...

Maybe it was a sign. It was too soon after the delivery. Jillian had already gone through so much.

Then again, wasn't it time for her to find a little happiness? At least he hoped he could make her happy. What if she hated it? What if she said no? What if she ran out of here fuming mad and never spoke to him again?

"Found it."

"You did?" He snatched it out of her hand.

"Hey," she argued, "I was looking at that."

"No," he replied. "No, you weren't. Now." He wiped the ring off with the corner of his flannel shirt. "You stand up right here. And I'm going to do it right this time."

He propped up one knee. Any fancy words he wanted to say about how happy he'd been since he met her, how impressed he was with how strong she'd been after everything she'd gone through, any speech he thought he had half-formed in his brain vanished.

But maybe that was okay. They'd gotten to know each other so well, maybe he didn't need a whole lot of words.

He held up the ring, which glinted in the sunlight. "Will you?"

She smiled and nodded down at him. "Yeah." She held out her hand expectantly.

He hesitated.

"It's beautiful," she said, her hand still extended.

"Thanks."

He stared at the ground.

"Is something wrong?" she finally asked.

He lowered his voice even though Peaches and her baby were the only other living creatures in the barn.

"I don't know what finger to put it on," he confessed.

She slipped the ring on with a laugh, and before he could say anything else, she was in the hay pile beside him, sharing one of what he hoped would be many, many sweet kisses.

The barn door swung open. "Don't mean to rush you," Connie called in, "but did she say yes?"

Peaches bleated, and her baby made a dash for the door.

"Catch him," Connie yelled. "We don't want him loose with that big cake out."

Ricky reached out to grab the goat's leg, but he was too slow.

The next thing he heard were screams from the guests outside.

"Get that goat!" Connie was yelling as she hurried toward the lawn.

"Should we head out and see if we can help?" He smiled down at his fiancée, then helped her to her feet.

"Don't let him near the cake!" Connie shouted.

Ricky was partly out the door when he realized Jillian wasn't with him. "What's wrong?" he asked. "We've got a goat to catch."

She stepped toward him and crooned into his ear, "One more kiss first."

Ricky was happy to obey.

Made in the USA
Columbia, SC
31 August 2019